✳ Tim came out the other side to a street of shops, which were mostly closed. The tapping sound had long faded away. He was alone. He'd escaped.

Then he heard a tiny sound—like a match being struck. Before he could turn to look, he felt a rough grip on his shoulder.

"Gotcha!" A blond man yanked the neck of his sweatshirt so hard he dragged him off his board. It skidded out from under him.

"Hey!" Tim snapped. "Back off!"

The man continued to grip Tim's collar as he looked at him with a sly smile. Tim could tell there was no point in trying to elude this one. He was younger than the others.

"Hello, Tim," the man said. His gravelly voice sounded friendly, but all of Tim's senses were on high alert. How did these guys know his name? "The others will be here in a sec."

As if the man's words had made it happen, Tim was suddenly surrounded by all four men, all wearing trenchcoats. All a lot bigger than he was, he noticed.

A man with a dark-brimmed hat pulled low over his forehead stepped in closer. "Timothy Hunter, my associate asked you a question," he said. "Do you believe in magic?" ✳

the BOOKS of MAGIC *1
™

The Invitation

Carla Jablonski

Created by
Neil Gaiman and John Bolton

BOOKS FOR
VERTIGO
YOUNG ADULTS

eos

An Imprint of HarperCollinsPublishers

Eos is an imprint of HarperCollins Publishers.

Library of Congress Cataloging-in-Publication Data
Jablonski, Carla.
    The invitation / by Carla Jablonski ; created by Neil Gaiman and
John Bolton.
        p.   cm. — (The books of magic ; 1)
    Summary: Thirteen-year-old Tim discovers he may be the greatest
wizard of his time when four strangers introduce him to the world of
magic, taking him on a journey through the past, present, future, and
Faerie realms, where danger threatens at every turn.
    ISBN 0-06-447379-1 (pbk.)
    [1. Magic—Fiction. 2. Wizards—Fiction.] I. Gaiman, Neil.
II. Bolton, John. III. Title. IV. Series.
PZ7.J1285 In 2003   2002032800
[Fic]—dc21   CIP
                                                          AC

Typography by Henrietta Stern
❖

First Eos edition, 2003
Visit us on the World Wide Web!
www.harperteen.com
www.dccomics.com

For Carol and Margot,
my cohorts in the search for better
physics through magic. . . .

THE BOOKS OF MAGIC
An Introduction

by Neil Gaiman

WHEN I WAS STILL a teenager, only a few years older than Tim Hunter is in the book you are holding, I decided it was time to write my first novel. It was to be called *Wild Magic*, and it was to be set in a minor British Public School (which is to say, a private school), like the ones from which I had so recently escaped, only a minor British Public School that taught magic. It had a young hero named Richard Grenville, and a pair of wonderful villains who called themselves Mister Croup and Mister Vandemar. It was going to be a mixture of Ursula K. Le Guin's *A Wizard of Earthsea* and T. H. White's *The Sword in the Stone*, and, well, me, I suppose. That was the plan. It seemed to me that learning about magic was the perfect story, and I was sure I could really write convincingly about school.

I wrote about five pages of the book before I realized that I had absolutely no idea what I was doing, and I stopped. (Later, I learned that most books are actually written by people who have no idea what they are doing, but go on to finish writing the books anyway. I wish I'd known that then.)

Years passed. I got married, and had children of my own, and learned how to finish writing the things I'd started.

Then one day in 1988, the telephone rang.

It was an editor in America named Karen Berger. I had recently started writing a monthly comic called *The Sandman*, which Karen was editing, although no issues had yet been published. Karen had noticed that I combined a sort of trainspotterish knowledge of minor and arcane DC Comics characters with a bizarre facility for organizing them into something more or less coherent. And also, she had an idea.

"Would you write a comic," she asked, "that would be a history of magic in the DC Comics universe, covering the past and the present and the future? Sort of a Who's Who, but with a story? We could call it *The Books of Magic*."

I said, "No, thank you." I pointed out to her how silly an idea it was—a Who's Who and a history and a travel guide that was also a story. "Quite a ridiculous idea," I said, and she apologized for having suggested it.

In bed that night I hovered at the edge of

sleep, musing about Karen's call, and what a ridiculous idea it was. I mean . . . a story that would go from the beginning of time . . . to the end of time . . . and have someone meet all these strange people . . . and learn all about magic. . . .

Perhaps it wasn't so ridiculous. . . .

And then I sighed, certain that if I let myself sleep it would all be gone in the morning. I climbed out of bed and crept through the house back to my office, trying not to wake anyone in my hurry to start scribbling down ideas.

A boy. Yes. There had to be a boy. Someone smart and funny, something of an outsider, who would learn that he had the potential to be the greatest magician the world had ever seen—more powerful than Merlin. And four guides, to take him through the past, the present, through other worlds, through the future, serving the same function as the ghosts who accompany Ebenezer Scrooge through Charles Dickens's *A Christmas Carol.*

I thought for a moment about calling him Richard Grenville, after the hero of my book-I'd-never-written, but that seemed a rather too heroic name (the original Sir Richard Grenville was a sea-captain, adventurer, and explorer, after all). So I called him Tim, possibly because the Monty Python team had shown that Tim was an unlikely sort of name for an enchanter, or with faint memories of the hero of Margaret Storey's magical children's novel, *Timothy and Two Witches*. I thought perhaps his last name should be Seekings, and it was, in the first outline I sent to Karen—a faint tribute to John Masefield's haunting tale of magic and smugglers, *The Midnight Folk*. But Karen felt this was a bit literal, so he became, in one stroke of the pen, Tim Hunter.

And as Tim Hunter he sat up, blinked, wiped his glasses on his T-shirt, and set off into the world.

(I never actually got to use the minor British Public School that taught only magic in a story, and I suppose now I never will. But I was very pleased when Mr. Croup and Mr. Vandemar finally showed up in a story about life under London, called *Neverwhere*.)

John Bolton, the first artist to draw Tim, had a son named James who was just the right age and he became John's model for Tim, tousle-haired and bespectacled. And in 1990 the first four volumes of comics that became the first *Books of Magic* graphic novel were published.

Soon enough, it seemed, Tim had a monthly series of comics chronicling his adventures and misadventures, and the slow learning process he was to undergo, as initially chronicled by author

John Ney Reiber, who gave Tim a number of things—most importantly, Molly.

In this new series of novels-without-pictures, Carla Jablonski has set herself a challenging task: not only adapting Tim's stories, but also telling new ones, and through it all illuminating the saga of a young man who might just grow up to be the most powerful magician in the world. If, of course, he manages to live that long. . . .

Neil Gaiman
May 2002

Prologue

DUST. IT WAS EVERYWHERE. Grime streaked the walls; trapped clouds of stale cigarette smoke had long ago tinted their once white paint a dingy muddy-water brown. Faded paintings hung askew, as if they were too tired to hold themselves up. *What would be the point*? they seemed to sigh. *Who is ever here to look at us now*?

A long bar, pockmarked with time and cigarette burns, ran along one wall. Unlit candles hunched in sconces on the wall, burned halfway down and unlikely to ever flicker again. The last time anyone had visited this hidden location, seemingly out-of-time, this precinct had held other tenants. Before the money and the parties and the carefree celebrations moved out and desperation moved in. The neighborhood above had changed, leaving the once exclusive underground club abandoned by those who sought the new, the shiny, the clean.

Abandoned, but not empty.

Now, in this dimly lit basement of a boarded-up shop in a seedy neighborhood of London, four men in trench coats eyed each other warily. The tension crackled in the loaded silence. Respect, caution, old battles, and new challenges mingled in the shadows. Even to a casual observer it would have been clear that these four were not ordinary men. The very air around them was charged, and it seemed that even the dust avoided settling on their dark coats. But there would be no casual observers; these men were far too adept for that.

It had been decades since anyone had been down here, and no one outside could have imagined the faded opulence in the subterranean room. The building had passed through several hands; it was unlikely the current landlord ever saw the basement. The shop above had been boarded up for several years, left to rot. No one bothered peeking in through the windows, no one peered through the grates. It had been forgotten; then again, perhaps it had been concealed, cloaked. These gentlemen certainly knew their way around shadows.

A match was lit. The blond man, slouched against a wall, brought the tiny flame to the end of his cigarette and took a deep drag. Of the four, he was the most ambivalent, hesitant—and yet so much rested with him.

"I don't want anything to do with it." He exhaled his words in a swirl of smoke. He let the match burn nearly to his fingers and watched it wink out.

The tiny end of the cigarette glowed as the man took another slow drag. It was the only light in the room, other than the faint and fading afternoon sunlight that attempted to creep in through the streaks of dirt. But these men didn't need to see each other to communicate. They had spent more than enough time in and with darkness. Besides, each was skilled in his own way of seeing.

"Constantine." The man known only as the Stranger spoke toward the direction of the cigarette. His voice resonated with authority but betrayed no impatience, since he knew John Constantine always presented a challenge. Particularly to authority. It was a quality that made him very valuable. "I thought I had made myself perfectly clear. We have no choice."

"Why not?" Constantine demanded. "And don't let's start debating bloody free will again, 'cause we could be here all week."

Dr. Occult turned from where he'd been peering through the streaked windows and cleared his throat. "I think what our friend is saying—"

Constantine cut him off sharply. "Not *my* friend, mate. Not these days." The edge in his voice could have sharpened a blade.

The Stranger and Dr. Occult exchanged a glance.

"If I might be permitted to finish, Mr.

Constantine . . . what our friend is trying to say is simply this: The boy is a natural force, for good or for evil. And it is up to us to channel that force for good and, perhaps, for magic."

When he was done speaking, Dr. Occult gave the Stranger another glance, wondering how his words would be received. Constantine took another long pull on the cigarette and said nothing.

The others knew better than to try and predict Constantine's reaction, or to take his allegiances for granted. It was never wise to take *anything* for granted with Constantine.

The fourth man emerged from the shadows, his blind eyes hidden behind dark glasses. "I say we should kill him," Mister E declared. "End the matter there."

The energy in the room changed; Mister E sensed their disapproval. The three others were in agreement against him. He did not like the odds, but he disapproved of their positions and would press his argument further. He knew he was right in this. They were foolish, soft. He could guide them. It was his duty to do so.

"As righteous souls, it is our responsibility to terminate the matter," Mister E said. Surely they could see his wisdom. It was so obvious, even for these morally ambivalent three. "We must ensure that this power does not fall into the wrong hands."

"There will be no killing," the Stranger insisted. He kept his voice neutral. "Our role is only to educate, to offer him the choice."

"Does one offer a rabid dog a choice?" demanded Mister E.

"That has nothing to do with it, E. The boy is no dog." The Stranger's voice hardened and his square jaw clenched. "He is a human child. A normal human child."

"Normal?"

"Why can't we just leave well enough alone?" Constantine moved deeper into the room. "If the kid's going to be magical, he'll get there on his own. He doesn't need us."

"Constantine, if he is to choose the path of magic, then he must choose responsibly," the Stranger said. He knew Constantine was aware of this; still, it was necessary to state it. "He must know enough about the labyrinth to walk a true path through it."

"And there are also those who would desire to show him another path," Dr. Occult warned. "The Cold Flame know about him already. My sources tell me they are still debating what to do."

"How do you know this, Occult?" asked Mister E. Suspicion made his unseeing eyes twitch behind their glasses. "Do you commune with the forces of darkness?"

Dr. Occult took no offense; he was used to Mister E. "You see traitors in every shadow, E," he said without rancor. "I have sources. I'd rather leave it at that for now."

Constantine hoisted himself up onto the bar, his feet dangling over the edge like a kid's. "All we know for sure is that we don't know anything for sure."

To the Stranger, Constantine's childish posture was mirrored in his adolescent statement. "That is a particularly foolish thing to say, John Constantine." The Stranger was beginning to tire of this debate. "Light and darkness, life and death. These things are eternally certain."

Constantine sighed. "All right. I'm not going to argue with you anymore, chief. What are you proposing that we do?"

The Stranger almost smiled; Constantine could seem positively petulant when he had to give in.

"Enlighten the child," said the Stranger. "Show him what magic truly is, and what it was, and what it may become. He has the potential to become the most powerful human adept of this age. It is up to the four of us to ensure that he chooses his path wisely. That is our mission and our burden." He let this statement resonate in the gloom. "Are we all in agreement?" He turned to where Dr. Occult stood by the windows. "Doctor?"

"I agree," Dr. Occult replied with a sharp nod. "I will show him the fair lands."

"Mister E?"

"If you are too soft to dispose of him, then I suppose you must educate him. If he gets that far, then I will take him to the end."

"Constantine?"

Constantine leaned forward, rested his elbows on his knees, and tilted his head. He gave the Stranger a squinty stare, then said, "Yeah, fair enough." He hopped down off the bar. "I'll give him the grand tour. Introduce him to the runners, give him an idea of the starting price."

"Then we are agreed," the Stranger stated. "It will begin with me. I will show him the origins and history of magic."

A crackle of electric anticipation circled the men.

"Let us go."

Three of them headed to the door that only they could find. Constantine lingered a moment, savoring the last of his cigarette.

"Just what the world needs," he muttered, dropping the butt to the floor and grinding it into the layers of time that had already accumulated, "the charge of the Trenchcoat Brigade."

Chapter One

What is the point of all this gross national product nonsense? What's it to me what the leading export of Chile is? There are some things I'd like to export <u>to</u> Chile, like Bobby Saunders for starters, but nobody's asking me, are they? No one ever does.

Does school have to be so boring? Is it a council requirement? There must be something vaguely interesting lurking inside all those books. Someone was interested enough to write them. Molly is bored too, I can tell from the way she's swirling her pencil around—she must be doodling in the margins of her notes, like she always does. Why can't *we ever learn anything interesting, answers to the really important questions, like why things are so bloody random, or how is it decided who is born poor and who's born rich? And why are the wrong people always in charge? But school's no place to ask such dangerous questions.*

Timothy Hunter pushed his glasses back up the bridge of his nose and tried to pay attention. No such luck. Social studies just could not hold his interest. Not when there were much more interesting things just outside the window. *Or maybe not*, he thought, his gaze sliding over the empty schoolyard, the chain-link fence, the broken streetlamp at the corner.

What is Molly doing now? Tim glanced behind him as Mr. Carstairs drew a graph on the board. Molly had the strangest smile on her face, so Tim knew she wasn't writing down the facts and figures that Mr. Carstairs was droning on about. *Of course, neither am I*, he thought, flipping forward in his notebook to find a blank page. If Carstairs strolled up and down the rows, Tim didn't want the teacher to spot his journal entry.

Tim bent his head as if he were writing intently,

and snuck another peek at Molly by peering under the crook of his elbow. Something was different about Molly this year. He had known her all his life, had spent many years trying to rid himself of her—but she didn't irritate him the way so many other people did these days. Lately, she was the only person he wanted to talk to, and one of the few he didn't mind letting into the flat when his father was home. Which was most of the time, since Dad rarely left his overstuffed recliner.

Maybe it isn't Molly who's changed, Tim mused. *Maybe it's me.*

Nothing seemed to fit these days—and not just because he'd outgrown his trainers and hadn't yet managed to approach Dad to arrange for new ones. Tim felt restless all the time, as if he had grown on the inside and his outside didn't have the room to accommodate his new size. But some days he felt just the opposite: that on the outside he had grown to official teenagerhood— thir*teen* after all!—while he felt smaller inside, and as skinless as a snail popped out of his shell. No wonder he couldn't find shoes that fit.

You truly are daft. Tim gave his head a sharp shake as if to clear it. *Molly was right.* One of these days he would think so hard his brain would explode. He told himself to time it right, like during a pop quiz. At least then the whole class would benefit from his early and dramatic demise.

The bell rang and Molly swung her head up to look at him. Her dark thick hair slid over one narrow shoulder. She rolled her brown eyes as if to say, "What took those bells so long?" and got out of her seat. She grabbed her books and bounced up to his desk, waiting for Tim to join her for the walk home.

It was over. The day was over. The week was over. There was an entire weekend of freedom to look forward to. Not that Tim had any plans. Not like there was anything to do. But at least he could go anywhere, be anywhere, at any time he chose. Well, that wasn't precisely true. With empty pockets and a curfew, his horizons were somewhat limited.

But there were the streets, and the docks, and the empty lots, and the whole grimy gray of London, unsupervised and unregimented—no bells ringing to demand that he move on to the next subject. He could read, he could write, he could dream, he could float away in his head to anywhere. And he could get there even faster on his skateboard.

"What's holding you up?" Molly said. "Molasses under your desk?"

Tim grabbed his books and leaped to his feet. "Let's blow this pop stand," he said, quoting the American gangster movie his dad had watched the night before on television.

"What's a pop stand?" Molly asked, as they bounded down the school steps.

"Dunno," Tim admitted. "I think it just means 'Let's get out of here.'"

"I'm for that!" Molly replied enthusiastically.

"Got plans for the weekend?" Tim asked. Molly came from a big family, so she was often busy at home.

"Well, let me see. I believe first I'm scheduled to address Parliament, ushering in some new laws. Then I have a ball with Her Highness the queen. After that I suppose I'll take the wee ones to the doctor while my mother and father take care of the old'uns and shopping."

"What a social life," Tim said with a laugh. He pulled his yo-yo out of his pocket and walked-the-dog, and did an around-the-world as they strolled toward home. Molly lived a few blocks farther than him, so they reached his house first.

"How about you?" Molly asked as they stood at the edge of Tim's walk. She twisted the end of her long hair between her fingers.

Tim shrugged. "You know. The usual. Watch grass grow. Watch dust collect on Dad."

"Ring me if you like," Molly said. "I'd love to see if grass could grow on your dad and dust collect on the lawn!"

Tim laughed. "Now that would be a trick."

"Oh no," Molly argued with an impish grin. "The real trick is avoiding death by boredom."

"'Boring' is one word that doesn't come to mind when I think of you, Mol," Tim said.

"Yeah?" Molly asked.

"Yeah," Tim said.

Molly always came up with crazy, cool ideas for adventures. Most of them were in her imagination, but they were exciting, entertaining. Tim enjoyed escaping with Molly into her wild stories.

A light blush crept into her pale cheeks. "See you," she said hastily, and walked away.

"Yeah, see you," Tim called after her. He slipped his yo-yo back into his pocket, took a deep breath, and braced himself to head inside.

For three years, ever since his mother died in the car accident—the one that left his father with one arm—his dad had had a deep relationship with drink and melancholy. Still, Tim always hoped to find something different whenever he opened the front door, or each time he came down the stairs. But his dad never changed, and it left him feeling foolish every time. What would it take to rouse his dad out of the world he now inhabited? A miracle. Or magic.

And what about me? Tim wondered as he opened the front door to the deep gloom inside.

He'd lost someone too, but his father acted as if he was the only one who'd suffered. Tim missed his mom with the same phantom feeling that he suspected his dad missed his arm, the same sudden shock of constantly rediscovering the absence. And Tim missed his dad too. This new version was a less than adequate replacement.

"You should see this girl's legs," Dad called from his chair in front of the telly, hearing Tim come in. "She was a looker, all right. They made films the *right* way back then." He tipped his beer bottle back, drained it, then added the bottle to the pile of empties beside the chair.

The living room was dark, the curtains drawn, as usual. The only light came from the vintage black-and-white movies on the BBC. Dad lived in a black-and-white world. Color had been drained out of the house. The curtains were never open, the lights rarely on. In the dim twilight in which they lived, there were only shadows and pale illumination—all in shades of gray.

"Yeah, Dad," Tim said, quickly climbing the stairs to his room. "Whatever you say."

Tim couldn't stand it. It was such a beautiful day outside; he couldn't stay cooped up with ghosts and permanent dankness. He grabbed his skateboard from its spot in the corner by his bed

and dashed downstairs again. Tucking it under his
arm, he swung the front door open.

"Going out?" his father called, his eyes never
leaving the set.

"For a while," Tim replied, and let the door
slam behind him.

He took in a deep breath. Autumn air, crisp
and bright, filled his lungs. He looked up and down
the street. No sign of Molly. Should he ride by her
home? He decided not to. He didn't want company
right now—he just wanted to move.

Tim put down the board and slowly pushed
himself along with one foot. This area of London
wasn't any more colorful than his home: the grit
of dirt piling up in abandoned lots, the gray of
the sidewalk, the institutional colors of the council flats, the tired gray faces of the unemployed,
their clothing washed so many times the color
had been leached completely out of it. There
were spots of black breaking up the monotony—
tar, grates, iron bars, and gates—but mostly it
was a gray world of cement, of exhaustion, of
dashed dreams. Of reality.

At least he could escape on his board.

Tim picked up speed and crouched low,
angling against the curbs. He felt a breeze swoop
in, ruffling his dark hair. The world blurred, and

now what stood out against the grimy backdrop were the few spots of color: Mrs. Waltham's hydrangea plant; tossed cigarette wrappers and junk food packets, shiny and bright in the gutter; a blue car, a red car, a yellow car parked outside the bingo parlor. At the speed he was moving, the world could be imagined as pretty.

Tim headed south, past his favorite old junk lot. He knew all the best places—empty, broken-down streets where he wouldn't have to worry about cars or pedestrians. Where he could pick up speed and test out new moves. He stood, held out his arms, and shouted, "Awesome!" in his best— or worst—American accent, imagining the surf splashing against his face.

Laughing, and glad no one was there to see him, he stopped to set up the right angle to take the ramp. He was going to grab some air!

Suddenly, he heard a strange tapping sound and glanced around. He couldn't tell where it was coming from, and figured it must be something banging against a building. He placed the board and took the ramp, executing a perfect twist-about as he landed.

"All right!" he cried, pumping his fist in the air. Too bad he *hadn't* invited Molly along—she would have been impressed.

Exhilarated, he rolled to a stop and tugged the end of his T-shirt up to wipe the sweat from his face. He was breathing harder now.

His head jerked up. It was the tapping sound again, getting louder. *That's no tree branch,* he thought. It was getting closer.

Uncertainly, Tim slowly pushed himself forward on his board. The sound now seemed to come from everywhere—it echoed around him. There was no way he could locate the source. He rolled to a stop, feeling a strange sense of dread.

A hand suddenly clutched his shoulder, and he whirled around to see a blind man with a cane looming over him, his hair streaked with silver at the temples.

"Do you believe in magic?" the man demanded.

"Get off!" Tim shouted, jerking himself out of the man's grip. He leaped onto his board and moved out, fast. The man was no match for the best boarder ever, a skateboard superhero, the Olympian of all skaters—

Whoa! He skidded to a stop. Another man in a trench coat emerged from the shadows of the overpass. "Tim," the man said. "We only want to talk to you."

Tim flipped the board, expertly turning

around, and pushed himself back up to speed. His mind raced as fast as his board. *How'd he know my name?* he wondered with a shiver.

Tim took a sharp turn, scooted down an alley, then pulled up short again. Yet another man in a trench coat was standing by the garbage cans at the end. *Nobody mentioned the freak show was in town.* Tim bent down, gripped his board, and did a fast U-ie out of there.

That makes three, he thought. His heart was pounding. *They were everywhere.* He wasn't frightened, though. Instead, he was excited by the chase, by the potential for danger, safe in the knowledge that these old geezers in their trench coats couldn't keep up with him.

Racing down a steep incline, he felt the breeze chill the sweat on his face. The freedom of the downhill move exhilarated him. "Can't catch me!" he cried.

He ducked low and spun into the loading area of the empty warehouse. He knew he could get away without being seen in here. *Nobody catches me,* he thought with pride. *Not cops, not weirdos, not teachers, not nobody!*

Tim came out the other side to a street of shops, which were mostly closed. The tapping sound had long faded away. He was alone. He'd escaped.

Then he heard a tiny sound—like a match being struck. Before he could turn to look, he felt a rough grip on his shoulder.

"Gotcha!" A blond man yanked the neck of his sweatshirt so hard he dragged him off his board. It skidded out from under him.

"Hey!" Tim snapped. "Back off!"

The man continued to grip Tim's collar as he looked at him with a sly smile. Tim could tell there was no point in trying to elude this one. He was younger than the others.

"Hello, Tim," the man said. His gravelly voice sounded friendly, but all of Tim's senses were on high alert.

The man's blue eyes flicked to the sidewalk. "Nice board you got there." He took a drag of the cigarette he'd lit before.

Tim squirmed, struggling to get out of his grip. He knew he probably couldn't escape, but he didn't want the man to know that he knew.

In fact, the blond man didn't even seem to notice that he was being struggled against. "Now, don't try to bite me, Tim," he said amiably. "There are things in my bloodstream you really don't want in your mouth."

What was that supposed to mean? Tim stopped struggling.

"We're not going to hurt you," the man continued. "We just want a word with you, see?"

Tim couldn't place the accent, though he guessed the man wasn't from a posh neighborhood. "Who are you?" he demanded. "Police?"

He knew he'd never done anything that would cause the police to come after him, but he kind of liked the idea that perhaps he was a suspect. It made him feel dangerous and interesting.

"Nah. I'm a private operator," the blond man said. "So are the other three." He smiled as if he was telling a joke. "About as private as you can get, in the usual run of things."

He released Tim then, and leaned back against a brick wall. He studied Tim as if he were some kind of specimen. It made Tim feel self-conscious; he ran his hand through his shaggy hair and wondered if he needed a haircut.

The blond man's hair was cut short, and his narrow face had deep creases. Tim guessed he was nearly forty. Either that or he'd lived a whole lot.

What did they want with him? Was he in trouble? Maybe they were gangsters and they wanted to use him in some crime spree—in a no-one-would-suspect-a-kid setup.

What should I do if they want me to rob a bank with them or something? Tim felt his pulse race.

The blond man must have sensed that Tim was becoming more agitated rather than less. "Relax," he said. "We're not here to hurt you. There won't be any trouble. Well, not of the kind you're imagining."

Tim flushed. He wondered what scenarios the man thought he'd been running in his head.

"The others will be here in a sec."

As if the man's words had made it happen, Tim was suddenly surrounded by all four men, all in trench coats. All a lot bigger than he was, he noticed.

A man with a dark-brimmed hat pulled low over his forehead stepped in closer. He had a strong, square face, but the hat shadowed his eyes. "Timothy Hunter, my associate asked you a question," he said. "Do you believe in magic?" He spoke like a headmaster, as if he was accustomed to be in charge. It annoyed Tim.

That and the daft question. *These guys sure are bozos.*

"Yeah," Tim retorted. "And I believe in the tooth fairy and the Loch Ness monster, as well." Tim crossed his arms defiantly. "Don't be stupid."

"I am not stupid," the man said. He didn't sound mad, just like he wanted an answer. "I'll ask you again: Do you believe in magic?"

All four men focused their attention on Tim.

Their intensity made a tiny trickle of sweat tickle under his scalp. They were serious. He decided if he kept talking back he'd never ditch these losers. He thought about the question and decided to answer it honestly.

"I . . . I did when I was a kid. And sometimes I wish there were magic. It would make things . . . I dunno . . . better? Weirder? More exciting?" He dropped his gaze and stared at his feet. "But it's like Father Christmas, isn't it? You grow up and discover there's no such thing." Tim shoved his hands into his pockets. He fiddled with the loose change, his keys, his yo-yo.

"Child, magic does exist."

Tim looked up. He could see white hair peeking out from under the hat. This one seemed to be the oldest of the group. No wonder he sounded so much like a headmaster. "There are powers and forces and realms beyond the fields you know."

Tim snorted. "I don't know any fields," he said. "I'm a city boy."

"When I say '*fields*,' child, I do not mean—"

The blond man gave a sharp laugh and grinned at Tim. "Don't you know when someone's winding you up?" he taunted the white-haired man. He turned to Tim, humor glinting in his blue eyes. "You're okay, kid. We haven't been properly introduced. I'm John Constantine."

Tim found himself warming to this one. Something about his attitude made him seem . . . cool. Like nothing fazed him. The way Tim hoped he'd be by the time he got to secondary school. "Uh, hello. I'm Tim Hunter."

"Yeah." John Constantine dropped his cigarette and stubbed it out. "First rule of magic—don't let anybody know your real name. Names have power."

"You told me your name, though," Tim argued.

"Did I?" Constantine gave him a wry smile and a wink. "Don't forget there's a difference between a person's *name* and what they're *called*. We know that you are called Timothy Hunter, but if that's not your true name, it can't be used to wield power over you. Anyway, perhaps I'm just along for the ride. Not like these three." He jerked his head, indicating the other three men, each more serious than the next.

Tim pulled the yo-yo from his pocket and started playing with it. He wanted to seem as casual as John Constantine. "So, what's your name, then?" he asked the man standing beside him.

"Weren't you listening?" the man admonished him. This one also wore a brimmed hat, but his hair was dark brown—darker than Tim's. "Never ask for a name. Instead, ask those you meet what they would like to be called. It will save you problems."

Tim rolled his eyes. He didn't need a lecture.

"Yeah? So what are you *called*?"

"Men call me Dr. Occult."

Tim wanted to ask what women called him, but decided against it. Instead he did another pass with his yo-yo and turned to the man on his other side.

Before Tim could even ask, the blind man said, "I am known as Mister E."

Some trick, Tim thought. *How'd he know that I was looking at him?* Maybe he wasn't really blind. Maybe it was an act. Then he realized what the man had claimed his name was.

"Mystery?" Tim said.

"Mister E," the man corrected.

How lame. "Did you make that up yourself?" Tim taunted. He turned to the white-haired man who seemed like a headmaster. "So, who are you?" he asked. "Professor Esoteric? Captain Nobody?"

"I claim neither a name nor a title, Timothy Hunter. Although I hope one day, perhaps, you will call me friend. Until that time I must remain a stranger."

This was all too much. They were so ponderous and heavy. They were up to something, but he couldn't begin to guess what it could be. He wished they would get on with it. "I don't believe any of this!" he exclaimed. "What's going on? Some kind of joke? Some twisted reality TV show?"

"No jokes," said the Stranger. "No tricks."

"We're here to give you a choice," Dr. Occult said. "Do you want magic in your life, child?" He crossed his arms over his chest and gazed down at Tim.

I'm surrounded by four loonies, Tim thought. "This is stupid. There's no such thing as magic." He flipped his yo-yo back up onto his palm and gave the four men a dismissive wave.

In a quick move, Dr. Occult snatched the yo-yo from his hand.

"Hey!"

Dr. Occult cupped the yo-yo between his palms. Tim's eyes widened as the man opened his hands and an owl appeared in a shimmer of light.

"Wh-What? That . . . b-b-but . . ." Tim sputtered. He watched as the owl flapped its powerful wings and flew up to perch on a window ledge above them. The owl held Tim's gaze for a moment, then Tim turned back to Dr. Occult.

"You . . . ? No." He shook his head firmly. "It was just a trick. A magic trick."

"No," John Constantine answered. "Not in the way you mean, anyway."

"Not a trick," Dr. Occult agreed. "But it *is* magic."

Tim looked up at the owl again. Amazing. One minute Dr. Occult held a plastic toy in his hands. Now a living, breathing bird stared down at them.

If I could do tricks like that, Tim thought, *Molly would be really impressed. And why stop with making birds out of toys?* With magic, he could get Molly's family a nanny, so Molly wouldn't always be stuck babysitting. He could make sure they always had enough to eat, and that her flat stayed clean even when her mum went a little funny. Magic could do a lot.

Tim felt excitement grow somewhere deep inside him, something that had been waiting to come out. He turned back to Dr. Occult. "Could I do that?"

The four men exchanged a silent look. Tim could not read it at all. They each wore different impenetrable expressions. Had he said something wrong?

The Stranger answered. "If that is the route you wish to walk, then yes."

Tim felt his heart pick up speed, the way it did when he grabbed air on his board and landed perfectly.

"That is why we are here," the Stranger continued. "Our role is to educate, Timothy. To show you the path of enchantment, of the art, of gramarye and glamour. Whether you choose to walk it afterward, that will be your own affair. Will you take this journey, Timothy Hunter?"

If I could do tricks like that, Tim thought, *they'd*

all have to treat me different. I wouldn't have to take any crap from anybody. Not ever. Not ever again.

He swallowed hard. He had no idea what it would mean to say yes—to keep talking to these weirdos. But he didn't care. He knew his answer.

"I'll come with you," Tim declared. "Show me what I have to do."

Chapter Two

TIM WAITED FOR THE men in trench coats to react. Instead there was a thick silence.

"I gave you your answer," Tim said. "Let's go." They had bugged him long enough—and now they were dragging their heels? It made no sense. Of course, he realized, none of this exactly made sense.

"He has given us his answer," the Stranger said. He seemed to be waiting for the other three to acknowledge this, but none of them said anything. Constantine dropped his cigarette butt and ground it under his heel. He shoved his hands into the pockets of his long trench coat. Dr. Occult nodded slowly and smiled, breaking up the strong planes of his face. Mister E stayed motionless, silent, with his mouth set in a firm, angry line.

The quiet made Tim nervous, but he wasn't going to let them see that. He stepped up to the Stranger. "So, where are we going?" he demanded.

"Through the door," the Stranger answered.

As if that answered anything. "Do you get paid for speaking in riddles or something?" Tim asked.

With a flutter of wings, the owl settled onto Tim's shoulder. Tim tried to duck away, startled by the sudden movement, but the owl clung to his sweatshirt, as if the bird were claiming him. "Ow," Tim complained. He twisted his neck to peer at it. "You need to have your nails clipped, Yo-yo."

"You've named him," Dr. Occult observed. "The bird is now yours."

"Of course he's mine," Tim declared brashly. "Didn't I skip Cadbury's Creams for three days to buy that yo-yo?"

The owl settled itself more comfortably on Tim's shoulder, and Tim began to relax under its weight. Not quite like a parrot on a pirate's shoulder, but the bird somehow felt right, sitting there. "Now about this door you mentioned," Tim said to the Stranger.

"The past is always knocking at the door, trying to break through into today," the Stranger said. "We will see the past, but we cannot influence it."

"Kind of like in that Christmas story with all the ghosts," Tim said. "Christmas Past, Christmas Future . . ."

Constantine chuckled. "But with better special effects," he said.

Tim grinned back. But then his smile froze. Behind the Stranger, blocking out a boarded-up billiards hall, a gigantic rectangle was materializing.

"Walk with me through the door," the Stranger invited him.

Tim was surprised. That was a door? It was a big block of . . . nothing. Just a large shape. It had no substance, no structure, only blankness.

The Stranger took a few steps toward the empty-looking rectangle. It was now at least three stories high, bigger than the building it blocked. Tim couldn't make his feet move.

"I—I'm scared," he whispered finally, knowing that the four men were waiting for him to do something. "I'm really scared." He ducked his head in shame. After all his bravado—his smart mouth that his teachers always complained about—after standing up to the these weirdos, and worst of all, after choosing the tempting possibility of learning magic, he now found himself unable to take a single step.

As if it sensed Tim's fear, the owl took off,

fluttering away. Its departure made Tim feel worse. Even his toy yo-yo was disgusted with him.

"Yes," the Stranger acknowledged. To Tim's relief, the man didn't sound angry or even disappointed. "You are afraid. There is nothing wrong with being afraid. It is not your feelings but your actions that matter."

Tim nodded. He didn't want to humiliate himself by backing out now. How could he live *that* down? For some reason, he wanted their respect. Particularly the blond one, that Constantine guy. Tim could feel his narrowed blue eyes on him.

One step at a time, Tim told himself. He moved his foot a few inches. His other foot followed. One step followed another until he found himself standing beside the Stranger at the edge of the "door." This close, Tim realized the Stranger towered over him by a good two feet. He hadn't seemed so large a moment ago. He also noticed that the Stranger's eyes were pure white! He had no pupils. Tim took a tiny step backward. What kind of being was he?

"If it is any reassurance," the Stranger said, "nothing can harm you. At least, not in the past. Ready?"

Too late to back out now. Tim nodded, shut his eyes, and stepped through the door.

"Agh!" He doubled over, his stomach twisting up inside him. He felt as if he were falling at a great speed. His entire frame felt stretched out and squashed, centrifugal force trying to flatten him like a pancake.

After what seemed an eternity, Tim abruptly felt like himself again. He could sense the Stranger behind him. They were floating in what seemed to be empty space. There was no sound. Nothing. Nothing but dark and silence.

"Where are we?" Tim asked. At least, he thought he asked, though he wasn't sure if he'd said anything out loud or just in his mind. In any event, the Stranger answered.

"This is no place, child. This is the void, the space before there was any *where* to travel to."

Tim tried to wrap his mind around that concept: *We're at the beginning of time?*

Then—Tim covered his ears. *That sound!* It was awful! Enormous! "What is it?" he cried.

"It is a cry of pain, child. The pain that comes with birth."

"Birth? Who's being born?"

"Not who," replied the Stranger.

"It's so loud. And it hurts!" Tim clutched his head, squeezing it hard, trying to push out the pain.

"Your pain is only the tiniest fraction of the pain that brought forth all that would become all. Time. Heat. Life. Everything."

"Everything?" Tim repeated. As intensely and immediately as it had invaded, the sounds and the pain stopped. Tim lowered his hands and looked around. "We're really at the beginning of everything?"

"In a manner of speaking. We are here as observers, not participants. Now, child, look upward. Do you see the silver city?"

Tim saw tiny sparks of light all around him. He was floating among the stars. He had no idea what was holding him up, or how he could breathe, but that didn't seem to matter. In the area the Stranger had indicated, there was a beautiful cluster of lights, swirling, moving, but all contained, like the most extraordinary constellation. He thought he could see castlelike structures, but it all kept moving, coming together, dancing apart, then coming together again.

"Watch closer."

Tim kept his focus on the constellation. Suddenly, there was a bright flash, a burst of light, of new colors raining down, scattering, breaking up the cluster. He wondered what had happened. It seemed that something exploded in the midst of the sparkling lights. Was it some sort of supernova?

"Wow! That's wicked," Tim said. John Constantine wasn't kidding about the special effects. "Like *Star Wars*."

"A strange analogy, child. But indeed there was a war in heaven and you see the vanquished now, burning as they fall, like stars. In the darkness before dawn, theirs was the first folly, theirs the first rebellion."

"What—What are you talking about?" Tim asked. "Whose rebellion?"

Some of the sparkling lights streaked past him, and Tim gasped. They weren't meteorites or spaceships—they were winged figures!

"They look like . . . angels."

"Precisely," the Stranger said.

Tim watched the angels fall, one after another. The Stranger named them as they dropped down: Lucifer, Uriel, Raphael, Michael, Saraquel, Gabriel, Raquel . . .

They looked so powerful, masculine, muscular. Tim felt puny beside them. He had always thought of angels as chubby little Cupids on valentines, or as Christmas ornaments, not anything like these creatures.

"They're so big!" he said.

The Stranger brought his face closer to Tim's, his white eyes glowing like the stars around them. It struck Tim that those white eyes were energy, and that the Stranger's human flesh was merely a container for it. "That is your perception. But, child, space is large, and there are many planes and viewpoints and dimensions."

"So you're saying they look big to me, but in the whole scheme of things, maybe they're not so huge?" Tim replied, trying to piece it together. "It all depends on your point of view?"

"Precisely." The Stranger straightened up again.

Tim felt as if he'd passed a pop quiz, and his forehead unfurrowed.

"Let's examine *your* world," the Stranger said. "See that star? That's your sun. Or it will be, eons hence."

This is unbelievable, Tim thought as he and the Stranger strolled through the night sky toward a glowing red sphere. *Is this really happening to me? Or is this all some wacko dream, and I'm lying in the gutter after being clonked on the head in a skateboard accident? Dad's always on me about wearing a helmet. I'd hate to prove him right.*

Tim once again felt a swirling, dropping sensation, his stomach leaping to his chest and back down. The skin on his face pressed against his bones, and he was certain anyone looking at him would be able to see his skeleton through his flesh. He could sense images, feel darkness battle light, and then light push it back. Energies of all kinds charged through him, but they were moving so quickly, he couldn't see anything clearly. The ether through which they moved was thick with souls—human, divine, demonic, animal—and all of them pressed against him, making him cry out, until he and the Stranger burst through the mass of entities into a brilliant blue sky.

They floated gently above an island of gems and crystal, glistening in the moonlight. "It's beautiful," Tim murmured. "Where are we?"

"We are about fifty thousand years before your time," the Stranger answered. "We are here to see the last and the greatest of the mage-lords of a land the people of your time scarcely believe existed. It was long since taken by the sea."

"Are you talking about Atlantis?" Tim asked incredulously. He watched as the waves below them began churning, sending up huge plumes of spray. "I thought that was just a fairy tale."

"You'll find that many a tale holds deep truth," the Stranger said.

Tidal waves rose up, smashing against the

glittering buildings below them. They were too far away to see details; all they saw were structures toppling, and Tim could feel the sadness and horror of destruction emanating from the doomed island.

"There," the Stranger said, pointing toward a small seated figure at the edge of a cliff. Thick mists obscured the cliff's bottom—and even the mountain it jutted from. *Or else*, Tim thought, *the cliff was floating in the air, like they were.* He and the Stranger approached, and Tim could see by the seated figure's change of posture that their presence had been detected.

The wizened old creature—he couldn't tell if it was male or female—seemed ancient. Wrinkles and very thin gray hair framed a thin and leathery face. The mage—for so the person seemed—wore a heavy tunic and sat cross-legged at the edge of the abyss, watching the beautiful city collapse into the ocean.

"What you have to understand about Atlantis is this . . ." The mage's voice quavered with age and emotion. "Are you listening, boy?"

Startled, Tim turned to the Stranger, who kept his white eyes forward, not responding to his confusion. Tim turned back to the mage. "Can you see me?" he asked.

"Of course I can't see you," the mage snapped. "But you ought to be here at this time, or so my spells have said."

Tim thought the ancient magician sounded cranky. He supposed that if he were that old, he'd be cranky too.

"Anyway," the mage continued, "where humanity gets it wrong, in your time, is in imagining Atlantis as having any kind of quantifiable existence. Which of course it hasn't. Not in the way they imagine, anyway. There have been many Atlantises, and there will be quite a few more. It's just a symbol. The true Atlantis is inside you. Just as it is inside all of us."

"What do you mean?" Tim asked. This creature spoke as enigmatically as the Stranger. *Do they all talk like this?* he wondered. "How can a city be inside us?" he asked.

"It is the sunken land lost beneath stories and myths. The place you visit in dreams and which occasionally breaks upon the shores of our conscious minds. Atlantis is the birthplace of civilization, the shadowland that is lost to us, but remains forever the true originator and true goal."

"You mean . . ." Tim said, trying to figure it out, "it's like what the Stranger said. That fairy tales can be true. Atlantis is just a name—for something else?"

"Close," the mage said. "Close enough for a start. It is a source. *The* source."

"Ooookay," Tim said uncertainly. He would just have to pretend he fully understood, otherwise they'd spend the rest of eternity trying to grasp this one concept. He could work it out later, the way he did with algebra.

"Now about the art itself," the ancient mage continued. "About magic. I think I speak with some authority here. I have lived for many, many years—more years than you can imagine. And I've had time to do a great deal of thinking. And what I think is this." The ancient creature turned his—or her—face straight in Tim's direction. Tim could see the eyes were red-rimmed—whether from weeping, age, or exhaustion, he could not tell.

"The whole thing is a crock," the mage said flatly. "Not worth the price I paid—not for one second!"

Surprised by the statement and the anger, Tim instinctively stepped backward. Why would the Stranger bring him to meet someone who obviously hated magic? Was this meant to be a warning?

The old creature looked into the distance. *Is the mage watching the scene in front of us*, Tim wondered, *or seeing memories of the past?*

"If I had my time over again, I'd be someone happy and ordinary and small. Never get involved in the affairs of the great and the powerful. Never discover the joy of the art. That's the trouble, you know." Again the ancient mage turned to face Tim directly. "Once you've begun to walk the path, there's no getting off it."

Another crash—and another sparkling building shattered and collapsed into the unrelenting sea below them. It seemed to dishearten the ancient one. "There. I've said enough. Take him away, Dark Walker. Show him the next exhibit in the waxwork gallery of the past. And, boy, don't take what they're offering. It's a crock—a big golden crock."

Tim watched, stunned, as the ancient magician's wrinkled flesh slowly dissolved, leaving only a skeleton. A strong wind whipped up, blowing the bones apart and then into dust. Within moments all that was left was a grinning skull. It was as if the only thing that had kept the creature alive was waiting for this conversation to occur. Now that the warning had been given, the magician could let go—and die.

Shaken, Tim stared at the empty eye sockets. "Did you know this was going to happen?" he asked the Stranger.

"Come, child," was the only response. "Let's lose ourselves into the past."

Lose is right, Tim thought, as images swirled by in a blur. He found himself in a cave then. The damp walls were covered in paintings of animals, illuminated by a crackling, spitting fire. Men in skins danced around the flames. Tim watched them trying to grapple with the dark world outside the cave: the mysterious forces that must be placated and persuaded, sacrificed and prayed to, loved and distrusted.

And so—there was magic. Tim wasn't sure how he knew this, but it came to him as truth.

Next, he felt as if he were in a museum of ghosts. Hieroglyphs of the dead surrounded him and the Stranger on the rough walls of the pyramids, and Tim realized that they had traveled to ancient Egypt. Dog-faced gods, azure scarab beetles, lotus flowers, and legions of painted men and women glowed from the walls. And magic was here too.

Then, abruptly, they stood on the banks of the Yellow River of China. In the sky, paper kites fluttered as priests ducked and twirled, wearing the masks of the sacred dragons. This too was magic.

The world shifted again, and Tim felt Mediterranean warmth, and sunlight. He was in an ancient Grecian vineyard, watching the revelers as they danced in a rite filled with merriment—and danger. Tim's body pulsed with the energy of the ritual, drawn into the compelling orbit of the vine and the blood.

He collapsed then, the energy completely drained out of him. "Stop it," he begged the Stranger. "Please stop it. It's too much." He lay gasping on what he thought might actually be solid ground. He knew he was alone again with the Stranger, the figures of the past vanishing back to wherever they belonged. Tim gulped and panted—it felt like they were still moving. "I think I'm going to be sick."

As if to prove his point, he rolled over and retched.

"I apologize, Timothy. I fear I have shown you too much, too fast."

Tim wiped his face on the grass, his mouth on his sleeve. He lay on his back and took in slow breaths.

"All those pictures. Those places. It's overwhelming." Even harder than the disorienting time shifts was the unbearable loneliness. Tim felt separate and apart from all he'd seen; observing, not participating. On the outskirts of events but not invited or included. It was too much like his own life back in East London.

And other than being reminded that he was on the outside looking in, what had he learned? All he knew about magic so far was that it had been around for a really long time, that people craved it, needed it, and yet in his very first encounter he had been warned against it—by the only person he'd been able to actually have a conversation with, a bitter million-year-old magician who instantly turned into a skeleton. *How can I learn what it is really all about this way?* Tim wondered. *Don't I have to do magic to understand it?*

"Isn't there anyone I can talk to," he asked the Stranger, "so I can ask what it's really like?"

The Stranger sighed. It sounded hollow and sad. "We are adrift in time, child. We have no more reality than the glimmer of a dream. There is no one with the power to see you. Except. Hmm . . ."

The Stranger appeared to have thought of something. Tim scrambled up—they had moved again. They were standing outside a thatched hut in a deep forest.

"Where are we?" Tim asked.

"Nearer to your time," the Stranger replied. "Close to Winchester, in England."

"Practically home."

They stepped into the hut, and the first thing that hit Tim was the odor. It stank! Some foul-smelling smoke rose from a cauldron hanging in the huge fireplace that took up one wall. Dried herbs hung from the mantel.

Across from the fireplace there were shelves lined with glass jars and thick books. The dirt floor had a large pentacle etched into it, with astrological signs running around the perimeter.

A boy just a few years older than Tim sat at a large oak table, pouring a thick green liquid into a small earthen bowl. He glanced up. "What took you so long?" he demanded.

"What?" Tim asked. "You were waiting for me?"

"I can't go on to the next step without those leaves," the boy said. "Did you have trouble finding the plants?"

"Uh . . . uh . . ." Tim stared at the boy, who seemed to think he was someone else. *Maybe the only way he can see me in his time frame is if he thinks I'm actually someone who belongs here.* Tim wasn't sure what to do.

"You don't have them, do you?" the boy said accusingly, rising from his seat. He wore a thick wool tunic belted over loose trousers, and short leather boots. Tim wondered who he was—then wondered *when* he was.

Irritated, the boy ran a hand through his thick blond hair. Tim could see that his long hair was none too clean. He didn't see a lavatory in this one-room hut; the boy probably bathed once a month, if that.

"I don't understand why they have paired us as apprentices," the boy complained. "Imagine, me, Merlin, with the likes of you. I am the most powerful magician of this age." He glanced at Tim and smirked. "Don't look so surprised. Even our master, Blaise, says as much. The magic burns in my veins."

Merlin came around the table toward Tim. He stopped a few feet away and stared at him. "But I sense the magic in you too," he said with surprise. "Something has changed you. An awakening. This power was not in you yesterday. Or even a few hours earlier when I sent you for the mugwort."

"I—I *am* different now," Tim said. That was certainly the truth.

Merlin nodded thoughtfully. "We should get back to work. We are still training, after all. Though why I should train when I know I will have all the power I could ever dream of . . ."

"Maybe that's how you learn to use all that power," Tim suggested.

Merlin looked at him sharply. "Yes, you have changed." He seemed to consider something, then said, "Why don't you work the next spell yourself?"

Chapter Three

TIM'S EYES WIDENED behind his glasses. "Me? Do a magic spell?"

Merlin shrugged. "Why not? You will have to work on your own sooner or later. Let's see if this change in you has any true merits."

Tim glanced back to see what the Stranger thought of this idea. But as usual, the man's face was expressionless. *Well, if there's any real danger, he probably wouldn't let me,* Tim reasoned, walking over to the oak table. *Unless this is a major test. Maybe I'm supposed to refuse. I could accidentally make Merlin disappear and then there would be no King Arthur, or Knights of the Round Table, and all the course of English history is forever changed. All because of me.*

Hmm. Tim scratched his head. *What to do?*

Merlin leaned against the bricks of the fireplace, warming his back in the chill air. His green eyes sparkled with challenge. "Afraid?" the teenage magician taunted.

Tim jutted out his chin. "No way. What should I do for my first trick? Make a rabbit pop out of a hat?"

Merlin looked confused. "Why would you want to do that when we trap rabbits right outside the door?"

"It was a joke," Tim muttered. "Sheesh."

"Make the potion on the next page. We can't finish mine anyway, since you neglected to bring back the mugwort," Merlin said.

Tim turned the heavy, grimy page of the book that lay open on the table. "To See in the Dark" was written in blue ink across the top. "Cool!" Tim exclaimed. What an awesome trick that would be!

"Yes, it is a cold night," Merlin said. "But that won't interfere with the spell."

This guy sure is literal, Tim thought. Then he realized that no one had started saying "cool" yet at this time in British history. "Forsooth, I mean," Tim tried. "This spell will be exciting."

Merlin smirked a little. "Yes, it will be. If you can create it correctly."

I'll show him, Tim thought. He read through the spell. Easy enough. He just had to blend a few ingredients while saying some weird words. How hard was that?

Carrying the heavy book with him to the shelf of jars, Tim looked up to find the first herb: couchgrass. He'd never heard of it and had no idea what it would look like. He hoped the jars were arranged in alphabetical order.

"No—No labels?" Tim squeaked. He glanced up and down the row. Not a single jar had a label on it identifying what was inside.

"We're not supposed to need labels," Merlin said. "You don't remember a single item, do you?" He crossed his arms over his chest and glared at Tim.

"Sure I do," Tim said defiantly. He balanced the book awkwardly in one hand and reached up for a jar. Then he stopped and lowered his hand. It could be dangerous to mix together ingredients he knew nothing about. He had learned that the hard way, when he and Molly blew up her chemistry set.

Tim hung his head. He was ashamed that he had even thought of trying to fake his way through, just because he wanted to show off in front of Merlin. But Merlin misread his expression.

"You have to study, lad," Merlin scolded. "That's the only way to learn. Don't be such a layabout. You must take magic seriously. It is a serious business."

"I will," Tim promised. "But there's plenty of

time to learn how to get these things right. I mean, my future is, well, in the future."

Merlin's eyes widened. "Are you a seer as well? Do you read the future as I do?"

Tim was stunned. "Can you do that?"

Merlin nodded. He took a bunch of dried herbs from a hook by the fireplace, crossed to the table, and began to grind them in a mortar with a pestle.

"What's going to happen?" Tim asked.

Merlin ground a bit harder. "It's all going to be a dreadful mess, really. I mean, I'll get Arthur up and running. Swords out of stones. All that."

Tim nodded, remembering the story. How astonishing to discover it was all real. And to be here before it had even begun.

"Create the fleeting wisp of glory called Camelot," Merlin said. He went to the jars and scooped a handful of sweet-smelling blossoms from one of them. He let them lie on the palm of his hand, gazing into them as if he were seeing the future in the delicate petals. "Camelot. It will be a glorious moment that sputters its light through the Dark Ages and then fades from sight."

He went back to the table and dropped the flowers into his work bowl. He crushed them under the pestle. "It would have all worked out fine if I could be there to see it through. But I won't be." Merlin worked harder, grinding his ingredients into a paste. His jaw clenched, his pressure on the pestle turning his knuckles white.

"Why not?" Tim asked, afraid these questions were making the boy magician angry. But he had to know.

"Nimue will come along and I'll go panting after her like a dog in heat. I'll teach her too little magic to do her any good, and too much for safety. All the while trying to get into her petticoats. Then she'll entice me into a cave and bind me there with my own magic and leave me to rot."

Merlin stopped to push his long hair out of his face. He stared down into the bowl sadly, but gradually a slow smile spread across his face. "Still," he said, turning to Tim with a grin. "It will all be very, very interesting."

"But if you know what's going to happen, why can't you change it?" Tim demanded. "Do it differently? Avoid this Nimue?"

Merlin seemed surprised by the questions. "I must do as I will do. Magic grants no freedoms. You know that. Everything it buys must be paid for." Merlin went back to the jars, running his finger along the shelf until he found the next ingredient.

Tim saw that Merlin was fading away, the whole room, the fire, the jars, all darkening—

returning to where they belonged in the past. And Tim found himself in limbo beside the Stranger once again.

"He was only my age," Tim said, his eyes still fixed on the spot where Merlin had stood only moments ago. "Just a bit older."

"Yes," the Stranger answered.

"Could I do what he did? Could I be as powerful as Merlin?"

"Powerful?" the Stranger repeated. "A strange word to use in connection with him."

"Why?" Tim asked. "Just because he ended up in some cave because of that girl? I'd be smarter than that!" Tim looked up at the Stranger again. "Can I be like him?"

"If you choose that path, yes, you could be the conduit for power that Merlin was."

"I'd like that!" Tim exclaimed.

The Stranger looked down at him for a long silent moment. "Perhaps you would."

Tim felt his heart race. This was big! His brows came together as he thought hard. He wanted to understand, not make mistakes. Tim remembered the force with which Merlin had mixed his potion, the edge in his voice as he described his future. "It seemed he was saying that he knew his life wasn't going to work out. I mean, he seemed pretty bothered by that. But he was going to do it all anyway!"

"Yes," the Stranger said. "That is what he seemed to be saying."

"The whole world knows about Merlin—*still*!" Tim went on, excited by the possibilities that were presenting themselves, fast and furious. "*That's* famous. This magic thing must be worth it, considering the sacrifice he ended up making." Tim held out his arms to the void, trying to feel its energy. "Imagine having all that power and being only a kid!" He turned back to face the Stranger. "Tell me more. Show me more. I want to see it all!"

Instantly, Tim doubled over again, but this time he was better prepared. He wasn't frightened or nauseous; his eagerness for experience knocked the dizziness right out of him.

Howls of fear and pain rose all around him. Tim gasped in horror. Women, and a few men, were being tortured in the dungeons of the Inquisition. Fire blazed everywhere, women screamed from wooden posts as they were set afire in Germany, in England, in America. Drownings, stonings, beatings, accusations, shrieks, cries, and wails clamored in his ears. Tim covered his eyes. "It's horrible!" he shouted above the din. "Horrible!"

"The burning times," the Stranger said. "They reappear throughout history. In what has been called the Dark Ages, but also in ages of so-called 'enlightenment.'"

"Why?" Tim demanded, sinking to his knees.

"People kill what they fear," the Stranger explained. "And magic is a powerful force. It deserves to be respected. But it is mysterious, so it can be frightening."

Tim pulled his hands from his eyes and watched the images pile up, layering over each other. "Are they all evil?" Tim asked, watching as old and young, beautiful and disfigured, were all murdered in a myriad of socially sanctioned ways.

"No," the Stranger answered. "Evil exists and magic can be bent to its purpose. But these accused were rarely evil. In fact, they were often not magical beings at all."

"Then why . . . ?" Tim couldn't grasp it, the torture and murder of innocents. "Why?"

"It was an opportunity to be exploited. Those whom they did not understand, those of whom they did not approve, were all herded into slaughter."

The cries faded away. The images froze, then dissolved. Tim and the Stranger floated in blank and silent space again.

"After all this," Tim said, shaken by the violence he'd witnessed, "was it over for magic?"

"In the forests, and in the high places, and beside the great stones, the old religions and old memories endured."

Tim thought about the time his class studied the pillars of Stonehenge. His teacher had said they were erected on a sacred site. It was hard to imagine, since they'd become a big tourist attraction, but now Tim believed it.

"It doesn't seem like there's any real magic anymore," he said. "Not like there was. Where did it all go?"

"Magic hasn't been lost completely," the Stranger said. "'Misplaced' would, perhaps, be a more precise term. Many of the powers of Faerie left this plane for good. And as science arose it left little room for magic."

"Why?"

"Both are systems of belief," the Stranger explained. "Science believes in what is explainable, verifiable. Magic requires an ability to plunge into the unseen and unknown. The two are rarely compatible. In your world, science has become the shared reality."

"What are you saying? That magic died out by my time?" If there had been something to kick, Tim would have kicked it. *This is so unfair! Magic disappears just in time for me to miss out?*

"No, it hasn't died altogether. But wild magic, the kind of magic that is present in every thing, every leaf, every rock—that is a thing of the past.

And since there are always those who would burn anyone they perceive as witches, many true magicians have adopted new garb, avoiding recognition by disguising their plumage."

"So there are still magicians," Tim figured, "but they're going to be harder to find."

"Correct."

"I'm glad to know magic still exists," Tim said. "It would be dead depressing to think we'd killed it all off."

"The human race has nearly extinguished it more than once," the Stranger said. "But the power, the art, the talents, the blood-gifts have managed to burn even in embers, and inevitably it ignites again. Given the proper fuel."

"There doesn't seem to be much magic where I live," Tim complained. Then he brightened and gave the Stranger a grin. "I'd like to be the one who brings it back."

The Stranger paused, and seemed to be thinking.

"Your journey has only begun," he said. "By the end of your path, you will have the information to decide what it is you want. However, I have taken you as far as I can, child."

Once again the shimmering nothingness in the shape of a large rectangle materialized in front of them.

"Push through that door," the Stranger instructed. "Beyond it are monsters and saints and sinners and freaks more remarkable than anything you have seen on our travels through antiquity."

After all that Tim had seen, he wondered what waited for him on the other side of the door this time. Could it really be more exotic than Atlantis and Merlin and the Spanish Inquisition?

He took a deep breath and walked through the doorway.

Into present-day London.

Chapter Four

TIM SQUINTED IN THE bright light. After the dark of the past, the sunny autumn day was a shock to his system.

Glancing up the street, he saw that the three other men in trench coats were still lurking about. Constantine leaned against the dirty window, thumbing through a newspaper. The blind one, Mister E, paced up and down the sidewalk, muttering angrily, his cane clinking against the cobblestones. Dr. Occult had his hat pulled low over his face; Tim wondered if he was catching a few z's. It made him curious—how long had he been gone?

Constantine's head lifted, and he straightened up when he caught sight of Tim. "Hullo, kid," he said. "How was the past?"

The two other men moved in closer. Dr. Occult smiled, but the blind man's face stayed stony and impassive.

"Okay, I suppose," Tim replied. He thought back over all he had seen. "I learned stuff." He grinned. "I threw up."

Constantine took a few steps backward. "Try not to puke on my coat, then. It's hell to dry-clean." But Constantine smiled, so Tim knew the bloke was mostly joking. Mostly.

Constantine tossed his newspaper into a nearby rubbish bin. "Right. It's you and me, then. I'm going to take you around a bit. Introduce you to a few people."

After the intensity of the Stranger, Constantine seemed refreshingly casual. Still, Tim had no idea what to expect. He wished he had some way to prepare. He didn't want to look like a dork in front of John.

Tim glanced up and down the street; the other men were just standing there. Waiting. A movement over Tim's head caught his attention. The owl—his former toy yo-yo—traced slow figure eights in the air above them. Tim grinned, remembering the astonishing trick. The magic.

Constantine cocked his head. "You want to bring the owl along?" he asked.

"Um, sure," Tim replied. He'd like having his bird/toy companion with him, wherever they were going. "Come on, Yo-yo."

The bird swooped down and landed neatly on Tim's shoulder. "Smooth landing," he told the bird. "That's one trick we're getting down." The owl blinked its yellow eyes.

"Two tickets for the grand tour, then, with yours truly as the guide." Constantine rubbed his hands together.

"Where are we?" Tim asked. He glanced around him. This made no sense. Suddenly the street was gone, Yo-yo was gone, and they were sitting—

"It's an airplane," Constantine said. "Big metal thing. Flies through the air. Sends your luggage off in the opposite direction. Only we haven't got any luggage, so that's all right."

"I mean—how did we get here?" Tim asked. He raised himself up onto the armrests and looked around. Flight attendants chatted by the curtained food service station, people read and dozed and listened to headphones in their seats. Tim plopped back down. "The last thing I remember, we were in the shopping precinct, and you were saying—"

"I said I'd be introducing you to a few people," John finished for him. He took a sip of his drink. "Well, most of them live in America, so that's where we're going."

"But I don't remember anything," Tim protested. He leaned in close to John and whispered, "And I don't have a passport."

A pretty red-haired flight attendant worked her smiling way down the aisle. John watched her as she passed their row. "Me neither. I had a passport once, but I lost it. I keep meaning to get a new one, but I never get around to it."

"But how did we get onto the plane?" This was as weird as traveling through time with the Stranger. Maybe weirder—since now the strange events were happening in the "real" world. Then Tim thought of something else, and said, "What happens when we want to get off? Go through Customs and all that?"

John smoothed his hair and straightened his collar. "You worry too much," he told Tim.

"And where's Yo-yo?" Tim demanded. "You said I could bring him."

"Bring an owl on a plane? That would be daft. He'll be waiting for you when we arrive," Constantine assured him. He flipped up the seat-back tray, unfolded himself from the cramped airplane seat, and stood up. "We land in New York in half an hour. Now I'm off to chat up that rather nice lady flight attendant."

"Oh. Right." Tim settled back into his seat.

"You're a big help," he muttered. Taking off his glasses, he shut his eyes again and decided to just accept that everything was going to be strange from now on.

The pilot announced their descent into JFK Airport, and Tim put his glasses back on and peered down out the window. *That's America*, he thought. *New York City*. Excitement welled up inside him; he kept his eyes glued to the small window. *I wonder if it will be like in the movies.*

John came back to sit beside him. "Looks kinda pretty from up here, don't you think?" he said.

Tim nodded, not taking his eyes from the unfamiliar landscape below him. He could see skyscrapers and bridges and loads of traffic, all in miniature. The flight attendant had to remind him twice to buckle his seat belt for landing.

Tim pressed himself into the seat as the plane taxied to the gate. He had to work hard to not jump up and race out the door. He wanted to see it all—now! America! Land of cowboys, and Wall Streeters, and hip-hop artists, and the original Levi's 501s, and gangsters, and movies and millionaires. And New York City!

"Can we go?" he asked John the moment the seat belt light went out.

John grinned. "Slow down, mate. It'll still be there even if we don't trample the locals."

They squeezed easily down the narrow aisle, since they didn't have to wrestle with carry-on bags. Tim noticed the red-haired flight attendant give John's arm a little touch as they left the plane.

The airport was packed, jammed with people, announcements blaring over the loud-speakers. It was so huge! *How do people find their way around?* Tim wondered, looking around him, trying to take it all in. He'd wind up on a plane to Timbuktu instead of London if he had to find his way on his own. It was a good thing he was here with John. *Wait a minute! Where'd he go?*

Tim frantically scanned the airport, his heart beating. Then he spotted John beyond a big family having a reunion. *Don't be such a tourist,* Tim scolded himself. John had simply kept walking as he stood like an idiot gaping at the sights. Tim hurried to catch up, not wanting to get lost. *And this is just the airport*, he thought. *Wait until I get outside!*

"You know, when I was a kid," Constantine said, taking long-legged strides, as if he hadn't noticed that Tim had been missing, "maybe about your age, I thought America was a magic land. It's so big—and you'd hear all that stuff about super-heroes and you'd believe it, because it was America."

Tim darted around the long line waiting to be checked through Customs. What queue were he and John supposed to join? Tim glanced around, puzzled, but John kept talking and walking. Tim figured he knew what he was doing, and tried to keep up with the man's quick pace.

"I mean, when I was a kid, America was somewhere that anything could happen," John said. "They had all this incredible stuff, you know. Pizzas, and fire hydrants, and Hollywood, and the Empire State Building. And they had superheroes and magic and aliens, and I don't know what all."

John kept moving forward. Past customs, past luggage pickup. He was heading for the exit! Tim whipped his head around. Any minute now the police or immigration inspectors, or *somebody*, was going to stop them. Weren't they?

"Anyway, then I came out to America and dis-covered it was just like every movie or TV show or cliché about America you've ever heard or imagined. It's all here, somewhere. If you can imagine it."

"But that's good, isn't it?" Tim asked, puzzled by Constantine's disappointed tone.

John shrugged. "Me, I prefer England. I prefer to live in a country that's small and old and where no one would ever have the nerve to wear a cape in public. Whether they could leap tall buildings in a single bound or not."

The moment they stepped outside, John reached into his pocket and pulled out a pack of cigarettes. He lit one and inhaled deeply. "And they have the most primitive smoking regulations."

"Those things will kill you, you know," Tim scolded. "And don't think they make you look cool. They make you look like you have a death wish."

John took another long drag and grinned. "You're one for speaking what's on your mind, aren't you? I like that." He raised an eyebrow at Tim. "I *think*." He leaned against a pillar.

Tim leaned against a pillar too, mimicking John's posture. "How did we do that?" he asked.

"Do what?"

"Get through Immigration and Customs. All that. We just walked straight through!"

"Yeah?" John said, as if he hadn't noticed. He straightened up and took a few steps toward the curb. "Now you've got a new experience coming up."

Tim couldn't help noticing that John didn't answer his question, but he decided to drop it.

Finding out what was coming next seemed more important. "Don't tell me," he joked nervously. "I get initiated into the dark mysteries of lost Lemuria and ancient Mu?"

"You get to ride in a New York City taxicab!" John stepped off the curb and raised an arm. Instantly, a yellow car squealed to a stop in front of him. John stubbed out his cigarette and opened the door to the backseat. "Your chariot awaits, sir," he said to Tim.

Tim scrambled into the backseat. It was lumpy—a spring poked him and he shifted his weight, trying to find a spot that didn't hurt. John gave the driver an address, then settled back into the seat.

"Where are we going?" Tim asked, still trying to find a comfortable spot. Every time he did, the driver made some quick maneuver that sent him sliding one way or the other. He needed the seat belt more in the cab than he had on the airplane!

"We're going to see a friend of mine. She's going to be delighted to see us. Lovely lady."

The view outside the cab window changed. They were no longer on broad highways; they had crossed over a bridge and were now navigating tight and small streets. The buildings were shorter than Tim had expected; the skyscrapers he'd seen from the plane and along the drive were gone. This area of town reminded him of posh sections of London. "Where are we?"

"Greenwich Village. One of the older parts of New York."

"Who's your friend?" Tim asked.

"Calls herself Madame Xanadu. And here we are."

They got out of the cab and stood in front of a dark brownstone building.

"Top floor," John said.

"Aren't you going to call first?" Tim asked, following John up the narrow stairway. "See if she's home?"

"She'll enjoy the surprise," John assured him as he opened the apartment door—without even knocking, Tim noted with surprise. He had thought that everyone locked their doors in New York City. John must be really serious about wanting to surprise this Madame X-adoodle, or whatever she was called. Tim stepped into a small alcove painted with astrological signs and strange creatures he couldn't identify.

The apartment was dark. A curtain separated the alcove from the rest of the place. Tim's nose wrinkled and his eyes smarted. Sweet and pungent incense sent thin trails of smoke wafting from burners set in the four corners of the room.

John pushed aside the curtain. A dark-haired woman sat at a round table, holding a deck of cards in her hands. Candles flickered from sconces on the wall; tapestries covered the ceiling, giving the room a tentlike look.

The woman didn't raise her eyes from the cards she was shuffling. "Enter freely and unafraid," she said.

"Madame X," John Constantine greeted her cheerily.

The woman's head shot up. *If looks could kill,* Tim thought. Daggers seemed to shoot from her blue eyes. "John Constantine," she snarled. "How dare you come into this place. Get out!"

"Looking lovely, as usual," Constantine said. Tim was amazed—he seemed awfully calm, considering how mad she was. "You haven't aged a day."

The woman rose from the table. "Do not attempt to flatter me, you—you sneak thief! If you think I've forgotten how you treated me the last time you were here . . ."

She came around the table and slowly stalked toward Constantine. Tim was aware of three things: the woman was beautiful, she was superangry, and Constantine didn't seemed fazed by any of it.

"You wormed your way into my confidence, purely in order to steal the Wind's Egg," she said, her deep voice resonating with fury. "I should rend you limb from limb. I should set harpies to tear out your eyes."

Tim shrank into the corner of the doorway, trying to make himself invisible. The woman clenched her fist, her bracelets jangling, her knuckles white above her multiple rings. She looked like she could do everything she threatened.

"How dare you step into my home, into my place of power. Why, I've a good mind to—"

John cut her off. "Would it help if I said I was sorry?"

Tim stared at him. He didn't actually sound sorry. Not exactly. He sounded more like a contrite teenager who was only sorry that he'd been caught.

Madame Xanadu wasn't buying it. *Points for her*, Tim thought. She put her hands on her curved hips, hugged tightly by her deep red dress. "I will give you ten seconds to get out of here. Then I will . . . I will . . ." She seemed to have trouble coming up with anything bad enough to do as punishment.

"Tim," Constantine said, never taking his eyes off the woman, "go and stand outside a sec, will you?"

Tim was relieved to get out of there. He didn't like it when people yelled at each other. His parents had never had arguments, so he wasn't used to it. Molly's parents fought all the time and it sometimes got really ugly. He didn't want to witness something like that between John and Madame Xanadu.

He pushed through the curtain and stepped out the front door into the hallway. He slid down the wall and sat cross-legged on the floor, wondering if the confused way he felt had to do with jet lag or with this strange adventure. What time zone was he in? He looked at his wrist and realized he wasn't wearing a watch. He laughed to himself. *You* are *out of it*.

A moment later the door to the apartment opened. Constantine popped his head out. "Come on, Tim. Let me introduce you properly."

Cautiously, Tim stepped back into the apartment. Madame Xanadu was sitting at the table again. She seemed a lot calmer. Tim wondered what Constantine had said to get her to stop being so mad.

Constantine put his hand on Tim's shoulder

and led him to the table. "Tim, this lady is called Madame Xanadu . . . Madame X, this is Tim Hunter."

The woman smiled. She was so beautiful, Tim couldn't help but stare. Her thick dark hair hung almost to her waist. Her dress was low-cut and tight, and left little to the imagination.

"I am pleased to meet you, child," she said. She gestured to the chair beside her. "Come sit. Constantine has told me a little about you. I will read your cards."

Tim looked up at Constantine uncertainly. "I—I don't know . . ."

John nodded. "Go ahead. These parlor tricks can be fun. Besides, I need to get in touch with a few people. You're safe here. A lot safer than I am," he added with a wink. He headed for the apartment door, leaving Tim alone with the beautiful Madame X.

"We will do the simplest of readings," she told Tim. "A four-card spread." She handed Tim the deck of tarot cards. Tim started—they tingled in his hands, like little electric shocks. "Shuffle them until you feel comfortable. Then lay out four cards on the table."

Tim did as she instructed. As he shuffled them, the tingling stopped and instead the cards

grew warm. He could swear they began to glow.
Must be a trick of the light, he told himself. All
those flickery candles.

"Hmm. All Major Arcana," Madame Xanadu
said, studying the cards Tim had set down on the
table.

"Is that good?" he asked.

"It's neither good nor bad," she said. "It just
indicates an intensity that doesn't surprise me."

Tim looked at the strange pictures, wondering how they could tell her anything.

Madame X laid a black-painted fingernail on
the first card. "This position tells us where you
have come from. You have drawn the Hermit. The
ancient one, one who observes. A wise man will—
no, has already—introduced you to secret knowledge. I see times gone. The past."

"That sounds like the Stranger!" Tim
exclaimed. "We were in the past!" Maybe there
was something to this Gypsy card-reading stuff
after all.

Madame Xanadu ignored him. Tim sat back
in his chair, hoping he hadn't broken some kind
of card-reading rules. *They should publish a
magic etiquette book*, he thought. *It would make
millions.*

"The second card tells us where you are right

now." A small smile crossed her face. "The Wheel of Fortune. What a surprise."

To Tim, she didn't sound surprised at all. But he didn't say anything this time.

She looked at him. "This is someone unreliable. A gambler. Adventure comes to you—adventure and danger." She tapped the card with her long fingernail. "That is what this card brings."

She looked back down at the table again. "The third card tells us where you are going. Ah. The Empress. This is usually a woman, but it could also be a man who is in touch with his female side." She cocked her head and narrowed her eyes, thinking. "But I sense more than one woman. Perhaps many. Women who will be of great importance to your safety—and your identity."

Tim nodded as if he understood, which he didn't at all. He was getting pretty good at faking it. He pointed at the last card. "What's this one mean?"

"It tells us where this all will take you. What this journey is about. Justice." She gazed at the card a long time, as if she wasn't just reading the name on it, but also trying to grasp a deeper meaning. "But I don't believe it represents righting wrongs in this card spread," she finally declared. "This is a decision that must be made.

Weighing all the information and trying to choose wisely."

She leaned back in her chair and shut her eyes. "Hmm. These cards might be conditions, or people . . ." She opened her eyes and looked at Tim, her enormous blue eyes serious. "I'm sorry, I can't be more specific. If we had more time . . ."

"Thanks," Tim said. "It was interesting— what you told me." It *was* interesting. Even if he didn't know what to make of any of it.

Her head flicked up. "But you must go. You ride the Wheel of Fortune. Travel with the gambler."

"Got that right," John Constantine said from the doorway. Tim hadn't heard him come in. "We need to be off now."

The urgency in Constantine's voice made Tim rise from the table quickly.

"One moment," Madame X said, standing up. "Usually I expect a gift from my querists. But in this case I have something for you." She raised her hand and an owl fluttered to her.

"Yo-yo!" Tim exclaimed. "Where did he come from?"

"It doesn't matter. He belongs with you."

The owl flew to Tim's shoulder. Tim liked how it felt there, now that he was used to the sharp talons. "Hey, Yo-yo," he cooed to the bird, which gave its feathers a quick ruffle and hooted.

"Right, then," Constantine said. "All set?"

Tim nodded, stroking Yo-yo's delicate brown feathers. The bird shut its eyes with pleasure.

Constantine turned to head out. "Take care, love," he called to Madame X over his shoulder. Without another glance back, he left the apartment.

"Uh, it was nice to meet you," Tim said to the woman. "Thanks for everything."

Madame X didn't answer. She just looked troubled. Tim wasn't sure if it was because of him, the card reading, or John Constantine. "So, uhm . . . 'bye," Tim said, then hurried to catch up with Constantine.

"She didn't seem very glad to see you," Tim observed as they went back down the stairs.

"I suppose you're right about that."

"Did you really steal her, what was it, Wind Egg?"

"In a manner of speaking," John admitted. "I meant to return it, but it got slightly damaged in a scuffle with a troll in Birmingham."

"Oh, sure," Tim scoffed. "There are trolls in Birmingham. Right."

"If you know where to look, yes." They

stepped outside and started walking quickly west. "Listen, we need to get out of here, and fast," John said. "I've received word that they're on to our whereabouts." He took a cigarette pack from his pocket. "I had figured we'd have a good week before they found us. Bad call."

"Do you have to smoke those filthy things?" Tim asked, theatrically waving smoke away with his hands. "And *who* are on to us?"

"The ones who want to kill you."

Tim stopped so suddenly that Yo-yo let out a screech and dug his talons into his shoulder more sharply. Tim ignored the pain. "*Kill* me? Why would anyone want to kill me?"

John turned to face him. "Think about it, kiddo. You are at the brink of serious power. You don't think people would kill for that? To extinguish it forever or to harness it for themselves? Either way, you've got a whole lot of people after you. And some of them aren't even people."

"Oh."

"Cheer up, Tim. Our side has plenty of muscle too." John started walking again, assuming that Tim would follow. He did, but it took a few blocks before he picked up his pace to match John's again. People wanting him dead was a bit much to process.

They strode along the city streets in silence. They'd gotten close to the river, and the neighborhood was fairly deserted. Most of the bars and restaurants were closed at that time of day, and people were probably at work. An old woman strolled by, walking a dog. A man in filthy clothes rummaged through a garbage can. Neither paid any attention to them. Tim had no idea where they were going, or if John had a destination in mind, but it seemed smart to keep moving. Yo-yo's bright eyes flicked from side to side as if he were keeping a sharp lookout.

"Listen, I just thought of something," Tim said. "My dad. Shouldn't I ring him or something? I mean, he'll be worried sick about me by now. And how am I going to explain that I'm in New York?"

"Don't worry about your dad," Constantine said. "The rest of the Trenchcoat Brigade will have taken care of that already."

"Taken care of . . . ?"

Constantine laughed. "Don't sound so ominous. They're just keeping track of the details, is all."

They turned a corner and passed a derelict slumped against the wall, a bottle of cheap booze beside him. Tim's nose wrinkled; the guy reeked. "Posh area," Tim commented wryly.

Suddenly, Yo-yo shrieked and leaped into the air.

"Look out, kiddo!" someone called.

Tim and Constantine whirled around as if they'd been choreographed. Tim's eyes widened in shock.

A beautiful woman in a flowing dress was standing behind him, brandishing a razor-sharp dagger—and it was aimed right at Tim!

Things happened fast—Yo-yo flew at the woman's face, and the drunk bum leaped to his feet, hitting the woman with his bottle. She slumped into his raggedy arms, dropping the dagger to the sidewalk.

"I'll take care of this one, Constantine," the derelict said, indicating the unconscious woman. "You need to take better care of the kid."

John grabbed Tim's arm and hurried him away. Tim's head swiveled around, to see what would happen next. But the derelict and the woman had both vanished. Yo-yo settled back down on his shoulders.

"What was that about?" Tim asked Constantine, who was walking briskly.

"Haven't the foggiest," his companion replied.

"But he knew your name!" Tim protested.

"My name?"

"What you're called, then," Tim grumbled. "And who was that lady? Was she one of the people who want to kill me?"

"We have to keep moving," Constantine said.

Tim shook his head. "I can't believe I'm having this conversation. I can't believe I'm walking along, uh . . ."

"Twelfth Street," John provided.

"Twelfth Street, with an owl on my shoulder. An owl that used to be a yo-yo. I don't believe I'm in America. I definitely don't believe that people are trying to kill me. I don't believe . . ."

"In magic?" Constantine stopped and turned to face Tim, his arms crossed over his chest.

They stood gazing at each other on the quiet street. Tim didn't know what to say, because he truly didn't know his own answer. He couldn't tell if John was angry or challenging or disappointed. He wanted his respect, and if John believed in this magic thing, then maybe he should too. *But not even John is perfect*, he thought as he coughed from some lingering cigarette smoke.

John broke the silence. "Look, we've got to get you someplace safe." He strode to a car parked at the curb and opened the door to the passenger side. "Get in," he instructed, then walked around the front of the car.

Tim's eyes widened. "Oh, bloody hell," he exclaimed. "Now you're stealing a car?" Tim was incredulous.

As if in answer, John opened the driver's side door.

"Are you sure you're one of the good guys?" Tim asked.

"I guess it all depends on who you ask. Are you getting in or aren't you?"

What choice did he have? He ducked into the front seat, and John slid in behind the wheel.

"Can you drive?" Constantine asked.

Tim laughed. "I'm only thirteen," he said.

"Oh well, I suppose it will have to be me, then." John turned the key in the ignition. He backed up and hit the car behind them, lurched forward and banged into the car in front. Then he jerked the car out into street. "Don't worry, it's not far."

Tim was stunned. How could a smooth guy like Constantine be this bad a driver!

"Where are we going?" He asked, quickly buckling his seat belt. He cringed as John drove too closely to the parked cars, smashing a side mirror as he went.

"San Francisco."

Tim's mouth dropped open. He swiveled inside his seat belt and stared at John. "But—

that's on the other side of the country!" His eyes flicked out the windshield. "Watch out for that car!" he shouted.

John made a sharp turn, barely avoiding an oncoming BMW. He pulled onto a main street. One with lots of cars. And trucks. And innocent pedestrians.

"San Francisco is thousands of miles away!" Tim exclaimed. "That trip would take ages, and I've got a chemistry test coming up! Plus I promised I'd ring Molly." He was about to explain that he couldn't possibly be away so long when Constantine's terrible driving distracted him. "On the right, John!" Tim yelled. "You're meant to drive on the right side of the road here in the States!"

"Tim, go to sleep." Constantine sounded annoyed.

"Huh?"

"Go to sleep."

Tim felt himself sink into darkness. He struggled to keep his eyes open, but it was as if there were weights attached to his eyelashes. It was a relief to let them fall.

All at once, Tim jolted awake, his heart pounding. He must have been dreaming—he had a terrible sense of danger, of a chase—a car chase, like in the movies. He blinked, shook his head trying to clear it, and blinked again. As the scene came into focus before him, sweat beaded on his forehead.

What am I doing here? He was standing on the edge of a cliff, and two cars were burning in the chasm far below him. Constantine was staring down too, and Yo-yo circled overhead. *Isn't that car the one* . . . His head whipped around. No car.

"Wh-What happened?" he asked John.

"A small disagreement over the placement of our cars on the road." Constantine sighed. His voice got serious. "They're still after us."

"Are you sure it wasn't your driving?" Tim asked.

Constantine grimaced at him. "I wish it had been. The sooner we get to San Francisco, the happier I'll be."

"Where are we now?" Tim asked, peering into the darkness around him. They seemed to be in the middle of nowhere.

"In Southern California."

Tim's mouth dropped open. *Wow. We seriously booked if we've made it all the way across the country in a single night.* Then he remembered his geography. San Francisco was in the north. And

California was a long skinny state. Their destination was still miles and miles away.

"Uh, we don't have a car anymore," Tim pointed out. "What are we going to do?"

"Stick out our thumbs, walk, and hope."

Chapter Five

TIM WAS TIRED, COLD, and hungry. His feet hurt. They'd been walking along this highway for ages. He shivered. Wasn't California supposed to be warm?

The few cars that passed kept going. Eyeing John's battered trench coat and dangling cigarette, and his own jeans and grimy T-shirt, it occurred to him that only a stark-raving loony would pick them up. And then where would they be?

"Can't you do something?" Tim asked.

"Like what?" John replied.

"I dunno . . . 'magic' things along."

"Doesn't work that way," John said. "At least, *I* don't work that way."

"Then how *does* it work?" Tim grumbled. "Aren't you supposed to be teaching me stuff?"

"You think you're not learning?"

Tim rolled his eyes. That wasn't an answer. He watched Yo-yo fly ahead and land on a tree branch and thought about the kind of magic that made Yo-yo. Reading cards was all well and good, but it wasn't the kind of magic that Merlin had. The kind he wanted.

"I want to—" Tim began.

"Catch that ride?" John cut him off.

Sure enough, a car had pulled to a stop up ahead of them.

"Quick!" Tim said, bounding forward. "Before he changes his mind!" He dashed to the car, Yo-yo flying behind him.

The driver had rolled down his window. A man in his forties stuck his head out. He was wearing conservative glasses, a long-sleeve shirt, and a sweater vest. "Need a ride?" he asked.

Tim had been wishing for a ride, but now that there was one in front of him, he felt uncertain. "Only if you aren't a weirdo trying to kill us," he blurted.

The guy laughed. "You're British, right?" he asked, obviously noting his accent.

Tim nodded. What did that have to do with anything?

"You Brits have such an offbeat sense of humor," he said. "Never fails to crack me up."

John had by now joined Tim. "Are we getting in?" he asked.

"Uh, yeah," Tim decided. With John along, he figured it was okay to accept the ride. He lifted his hand and Yo-yo landed on it.

"The bird too?" the driver asked.

"The bird too," Tim replied.

John sat up front next to the driver, while Tim sprawled across the backseat. Yo-yo perched behind John, balancing on the back of his seat. The car drove off.

"You tourists?" the driver asked.

"You might say that. I'm John Constantine." He jerked his head toward the backseat. "And this is Tim."

"Hi," Tim said, observing that the man was a much better driver than John. He started to relax. The man reminded him of American professors on television. "And the owl's name is Yo-yo." Yo-yo ducked his head as if saying hello.

"I'm Terrence Thirteen," the man said, introducing himself. "Dr. Terry Thirteen."

"The ghost-breaker?" John asked.

"You've heard of me?" Dr. Thirteen smiled.

"Yeah," John replied. "Read your book. Funny meeting you like this."

Tim sat up and rested his elbows on the front

seat rest, leaning between the two men. Could
John have somehow arranged this meeting? He
didn't think Constantine believed much in coincidence. He wondered what the man's book was
about. And if Thirteen was his real name.

The sky was brightening slightly, but it was
still dark. "Do you have an interest in the subject?"
Dr. Thirteen asked John as he navigated through
the ground fog that now surrounded them.

"Well, Tim here is sort of interested in magic.
You must have firm opinions on the subject."

Dr. Thirteen laughed. "You could say that."

"Why?" Tim asked. "What do you know about
magic?"

"Well, Tim, I've been investigating the occult
for fifteen years now. You know, magic, spooks,
witch cults. You might call me a professional
debunker."

"You mean you prove that they're fake?" This
surprised Tim. He gave John a quick glance. What
did he think of this?

"In fifteen years I haven't seen one thing that
didn't have a rational explanation. Either it was a
hoax, or a fraud, or—most often—people wanting
so much to believe in powerful forces that they'd
convinced themselves of the existence of magic.
They'd take simple coincidence or delusion as

proof of their superstitions."

Tim leaned back in his seat. "Fifteen years," he said, letting out a low whistle. "That's longer than I've been alive."

Dr. Thirteen grinned at Tim in the rearview mirror. "Yes, Tim. With all that experience, I think I can say with some certainty that if magic existed, I would have found some evidence of it by now. And I haven't."

Tim nodded slowly. Yesterday, he would have immediately agreed with Dr. Thirteen. But now . . . well, everything was different now.

Tim fell asleep for a while, and when he awoke, the sun had risen. He looked out the window and saw something he recognized—the Golden Gate Bridge. San Francisco already! Terry gave them a short tour—pointing out the old island prison of Alcatraz, the marina where yachts and house boats bobbed gently in the bay, and the Ghirardelli chocolate factory. He let them out at the Fisherman's Wharf turnaround. The whole area smelled strongly of fish and seaweed, and the calls of the seagulls seemed to make Yo-yo nervous. He dug his talons deeper into Tim's shoulder.

"Magic is a nice hobby if you're planning to entertain at a party," Dr. Thirteen told Tim, leaning out of his window. "But otherwise, don't waste your time on it."

"Thanks for the ride," Tim said.

Dr. Thirteen drove off. Tim watched him go, wondering how John would react to all that they'd heard.

"That bloke," John said. "He doesn't believe in magic at all. And he's right."

"What?" Tim's head snapped up so fast it startled Yo-yo, who took off into the air. "What do you mean, he's right?"

Constantine shrugged. "Magic doesn't exist. For him."

A cable car ground to a stop, and Tim and John helped the conductor and several prospective passengers turn it around, and then hopped aboard. Yo-yo flew alongside them. At this hour of the morning, with the sun just rising, the trolley was nearly empty.

"I don't understand," Tim said.

"You have to *choose* it, you see," John explained. He gave Tim a squinty, sidelong look. Tim wondered if John ever looked at anything straight on. "That's what we're offering you. The choice. If you don't want magic, you'll never see it again. You'll live in a rational world in which everything can be explained."

That doesn't sound so bad, Tim thought. What

was John trying to tell him? Or was he trying to tell him anything at all? It was hard to figure out.

"This is us," John said after they'd ridden awhile. He rang the bell and gracefully stepped off the cable car before it had come to a full stop. Tim scrambled after him. *The guy lopes along like a panther*, he thought.

"But if you choose it," John continued, as if he'd never stopped speaking, "well, it's like stepping off the sidewalk into the street. The world still looks the same on the surface, but you can be hit by a truck at any second. That's magic."

"But that sounds dangerous. Why would I want to do that?" Tim asked.

"I guess some people prefer life in the fast lane. But I'm not the one deciding. You are."

They walked along in near silence again. The only sound was the flapping of Yo-yo's wings. Then another sound: Tim's stomach growled. Loudly. How embarrassing. Tim slapped his hand over his stomach.

"You can have breakfast at our next port of call. And sanctuary too, with any luck," John promised with a grin.

"Are we dropping in unexpectedly on another one of your friends?" Tim asked.

"As it happens, yes."

"Oh, and that worked so well with Madame Xanadu," Tim scoffed. "No thanks."

"Zatanna isn't anything like Madame X," John said.

"Zatanna?" Tim repeated. His eyes widened as he looked up at John. "Zatanna the lady magician?"

"The very same," John replied.

"I've seen her on TV! She's brilliant! You know her?"

John smiled. "That's the first time you've actually sounded excited since we started this little journey," he said. "I've finally managed to impress you."

"Wait a minute," Tim stopped, suddenly anxious.

John gave him a quizzical look. "What are you worrying about now?"

"Well, it's just that, judging by the way things have gone so far, she's probably a loon who hates you."

"Nah, me and Zatanna go way back."

"Sure. I expect you probably pinched her best trick or something."

"This is her house," John said, ignoring Tim's comment. They were in a neighborhood of brightly painted houses, all colors of candy. He led Tim up the walk of a pink house with blue shutters. Large rosebushes lined the path.

Tim followed reluctantly. He admired Zatanna, and he wanted to keep it that way. He didn't want to discover that the real person wasn't quite as cool as the person he'd seen on TV. And he didn't want to get on her bad side by showing up at dawn *without* an invitation and *with* John Constantine. Even Yo-yo seemed hesitant. "Are you sure this is a good idea?"

John gave him a wicked grin. "What's the matter, kid, don't you trust me?" He rang the doorbell.

"At least we're not just barging in this time," Tim muttered. "She can slam the door in our faces if she wants."

A tall, dark-haired woman wearing a big T-shirt and leggings opened the door. She looked sleepy.

She took a minute to focus, then a huge grin spread across her face. "John? John Constantine! I can't believe it's you!" She threw her arms around him, gripping him in a great bear hug. "What brings you to San Francisco?"

"Hey, Zatanna."

Is that relief in his voice? Tim wondered. *It seemed John hadn't been quite as sure of his reception as he'd pretended.*

Zatanna released John and gave his arm a playful smack. "What has it been—two years?" She grinned at Tim. "So who's your buddy?"

Zatanna looked friendly, Tim observed. And a lot more normal than Madame X. She was a pretty woman, a little younger than John. She reminded Tim of a grown-up Molly.

"I'm Tim," he said. "Timothy," he corrected himself. Timothy sounded more grown-up. "Timothy Hunter. I saw you on Jonathan Ross."

Zatanna's brow furrowed, then her eyes showed that she remembered who Jonathan Ross was. "Oh right! Britain's answer to Letterman. That was fun. Come on in, you two."

Zatanna ushered them into her house. The hallway was painted a rosy pink, and wooden pegs held jackets, shoulder bags, hats, and colorful scarves. She brought them into a bright living room—sun streamed through the gauzy curtains, filling the room with light. Flower pots filled all the windows, and there were large plants nearly as big as trees in the corners. It was like walking into a garden. Yo-yo immediately made himself at home on the windowsill.

"It's so sunny here!" Tim blurted, feeling warmed by the light. After the gloom of London and the dark night of hitchhiking, Zatanna's living room was dazzling. Still, it seemed foolish to say out loud, and Tim flushed.

"Yeah, California is famous for it," Zatanna said. She didn't seem to take any notice of Tim's embarrassment. "Of course, San Francisco gets its share of rain and fog. That should make you feel right at home." She flopped onto a large futon that was covered with embroidered pillows.

"So Tim," she said, patting the spot on the couch beside her. Tim crossed to her and sat down. "What are you doing with my off-white knight in not-so-shining armor?" She gave John a mischievous grin. Tim could tell she enjoyed teasing John, and that he liked it. She seemed to be an equal match for Constantine.

John leaned against a bookshelf and waved a fern frond away from his face. "Tim has the potential to be the greatest magician that the modern world has ever seen. So me, Doc Occult, and the Stranger, along with the nut from Boston—"

"Who?"

"He calls himself Mister E."

"Oh, right. Him." She sounded dismissive, as if she didn't think much of Mister E. Tim tucked that bit of info away for future reference.

"Well, we got together and we're showing him stuff," John explained. "The idea being that he learns enough about the world of magic to decide whether that's what he wants from life or not."

Tim picked up a pillow and set it across his lap. He stared down at it, as if the embroidered flowers were the most fascinating things he'd ever seen.

There it was, then. All laid out. These four men—the "Trenchcoat Brigade," as Constantine called them—sought him out because he really and truly could become powerful. The *most* powerful. Bigger than Merlin even. But it was up to him to decide if that's what he wanted. Well, why wouldn't he?

"Sounds like fun," Zatanna said.

"Only trouble is, people are trying to kill him," John told her. "We're trying to find somewhere to hide that's safe, until the whole thing blows over."

Oh yeah. Tim remembered the part about people wanting to kill him. That put a damper on everything. *But if I'm so powerful,* he thought, *can't I protect myself from my enemies?* Though he supposed that if he could, they would have shown him how already.

"Why don't you guys stay here!" Zatanna said. She put a hand on Tim's arm. "I'd be delighted to have you."

Tim nodded a thank-you but couldn't quite meet her friendly smile. *What if it doesn't blow over?* Tim worried. Would he have to stay in hiding forever?

Zatanna must have sensed his discomfort, because she stood and changed the subject. "Oh— John. I just remembered, there's a letter for you on the table."

"Letter?" John seemed surprised.

"Yeah, the envelope was there when I came down this morning. Weird, huh?" She twisted her hair into a loose braid and grinned. "I suppose that should have warned me that the British were invading."

John crossed to the table, a puzzled expression on his face.

"Great-looking owl," Zatanna said to Tim. "Did you make him yourself?"

"No, Dr. Occult did," Tim admitted. If he was so magical, why couldn't he do a simple trick like that? He looked up at Zatanna. "I couldn't believe it when you made flowers grow out of Jonathan Ross's ears on TV," he said. "Can you teach me to do that?"

"Oh bloody hell," John sputtered. He whirled around so fast, the tails of his trench coat flapped. "Take care of Tim until I get back, can you, love?"

"What?" Tim asked.

"What?" Zatanna echoed.

John crumpled the letter and shoved it into

his pocket. "Honestly, I can't leave them alone for five minutes." He seemed really mad.

"John, where are you going?" Zatanna asked.

"India," John replied grimly. "Calcutta probably. See ya, darlin'. 'Bye, Tim. I'll be back as soon as I can." Without another word, he bolted out of the house.

Zatanna and Tim hurried to the front door after him. "India? How long will you be gone?" Zatanna called after John.

He gave a wave without turning around, and then vanished into the traffic.

"But what am I supposed to do with . . ." Zatanna's voice trailed off as she caught Tim's expression. She smiled and shrugged. "What's the use. He'll be back when he gets back, I suppose."

Tim didn't like the feeling that he was imposing. "Look, I'm really sorry about this. I can go."

"No," Zatanna insisted. She put a hand on his shoulder and firmly turned him around, shutting the door behind them. "You're only, what—thirteen years old? And they're trying to kill you. You shouldn't be on your own. Though you're a lot more grown-up than your pal Constantine," she added, ruffling his hair.

Tim laughed and felt relieved.

"Now, when was the last time you ate?" Zatanna asked.

"I'm not sure," Tim replied. "Traveling with Constantine, time goes really funny. If you know what I mean."

"Mmm. And I doubt you've had a shower since you left England. So if you head upstairs, you'll find the bathroom on your left, and I'll have breakfast ready for you when you come down. You can leave the owl with me. Now go."

Tim climbed the stairs. Pictures of Zatanna performing lined the upstairs hallway. *I'm in the house of a real celebrity*, he thought. *I wish I could tell Molly about this!*

The bathroom was full of pink and lavender soaps and bath salts and other girly things. Tim undressed, took off his glasses, and turned on the water. The faucets worked differently than in his home in London, but he soon figured out which was hot, which was cold, and how to adjust them. He let the water and steam pound the miles and confusion from his skin.

He stepped back out into the now steamy bathroom and wrapped himself in a towel. He didn't think he should borrow Zatanna's toothbrush, so he squirted some toothpaste onto his finger and rubbed his teeth with it.

"I've left clean clothes outside the door," Zatanna called through the bathroom door.

Tim spit into the sink. "Okay."

He waited until he heard her footsteps going down the stairs, then opened the door a crack and pulled the clothing into the bathroom. He dressed and went down to the kitchen.

"Um, this may be a silly question," he said, "but where did you get boys' clothes? In my size?"

"Magic," she said simply, as if that were the normal, expected answer.

"Oh."

Zatanna didn't elaborate, so Tim didn't ask anything else. He sat at the table. The kitchen was sunny too—and painted bright yellow, with stencils running up by the ceiling. Plants sat in pots here too, but he thought they might be the kind used in cooking, because the whole room smelled spicy. Zatanna stood at the stove, scrambling something in a pan. She expertly flipped it onto a plate and set it in front of him. Whatever it was, it smelled great!

"Okay, I've made you breakfast," she declared. "It's vegetarian, I'm afraid, but I think you'll like it. Yo-yo's asleep in the attic for the day."

"How did you know his name's Yo-yo?"

"Magic."

Tim left it at that and shoveled the food into his mouth. He had no idea how starved he actually was until he'd begun to eat. "This is absolutely incredible," he said, his mouth full.

"I wish my dad could cook like this. Did you make the food by magic?"

Zatanna laughed. It was a warm, friendly, full-out laugh. Not a little silly tee-hee or giggle. "No, I made it the regular way." She dropped the pan into the sink and turned on the water. "Say," she said, turning to face him. "Is there anyone you need to phone?"

"I dunno." He stared at the tines of his fork as if they would tell him what to do. "Maybe I should ring my dad. John said they'd taken care of all that, but I ought to let him know I'm okay."

"Sounds like a good idea," Zatanna said.

She went back to washing dishes, and Tim finished his veggie breakfast. He carried the plate to the sink. "Should I phone now?"

"No time like the present," Zatanna said. "There's a phone in the living room."

She explained how to dial an international call, and Tim went into the other room. He found the phone, punched in all the numbers, and listened to the comforting and familiar double ring of British Telecom.

"Hi, Dad," Tim said as soon his father picked up.

"Tim! How's Brighton?"

That's strange, Tim thought. *Why would he*

think I'm in Brighton? "I'm not in Brighton, Dad."
He took a deep breath, bracing himself for his
dad's shocked reaction. "I'm in San Francisco."

"Yeah, it's raining here as well. How's your
Auntie Blodwyn, then? And the kids?"

Tim held the phone away from his ear and
stared at it. It was as if his dad hadn't heard him
right. Or at all. Was there something wrong with
the connection? "I'm in San Francisco, Dad," he
repeated, louder. "I'm staying with Zatanna. You
know, the famous magician." His dad would know
who she was—they had watched her on television
together.

"Well, that's good. Don't lose too much
money on the pier. I know how much you love
the amusements there. I'll see you when you get
back, then. Cheers, lad."

"But Dad—"

Tim heard the click on the other end and his
dad was gone.

"How's your father?" Zatanna asked. She
stood in the doorway of the living room, light from
the kitchen streaming in behind her.

Tim continued to stare at the phone. "He
thinks I'm in Brighton. I told him I wasn't, and he
didn't hear me." He put the receiver back down
with a shaky hand. He didn't want Zatanna to see

him freak out, but the conversation had really unsettled him. "This is really weird." He tried to keep his voice steady, but it was hard. "I mean, it's okay when I'm with John. When you're with him, the weird stuff seems almost normal, you know?"

He looked at Zatanna to see if she understood what he meant. "I know," she said.

"But now that he's gone . . . I spoke to my dad and he didn't hear me, Zatanna." Tim sank down onto the futon. He didn't think his legs would hold him up anymore, they were shaking so hard. For the first time since this crazy adventure began, the first time since he stepped through that magical doorway, he felt really scared.

Zatanna sat down beside him and put an arm around his shoulders. "It's okay, Tim. It will all be fine," she assured him. "It's just all new. A lot to get used to. But you're not alone. Constantine will come back for you. He may seem unreliable and all that, but he will come back."

Tim pushed his glasses back up and nodded. She did understand how he was feeling—he was sure of it. He liked how it felt to have her hand on his arm and hear her speak so soothingly. It was like having his mom back for just a minute.

"Say—do you want to go to a party?" she asked. "You're under my protection and I won't let any harm come to you."

Tim looked up at her. "A party?"

"A Halloween party, to be precise!"

He grinned. "Wicked!"

"It should be fun. I got the invitation last night. I hadn't planned to go, but . . ." She gave his arm a pat. "I have to do my best to entertain my honored guest! Besides, John was planning to introduce you to some of the most prominent practitioners of magic in the country. I might as well take you out and show you a few more."

"Brilliant." Going to a party with a famous magician—a celebrity—that would be amazing! One for the scrapbook, that's for sure.

Zatanna stood up. "So why don't you take a nap. You must be exhausted from all this travel."

"Sounds good." She was right. Though he'd slept briefly in the car, every muscle in his body moaned for rest—and his brain would definitely welcome the opportunity to blink off.

"The guest room is right next to the bathroom. It's blue."

"Is every room in your house painted a different color?" Tim asked as he headed up the stairs.

"Yup," Zatanna answered. "And I change them all the time." She gave Tim a wink. "One of the benefits of magic. I can redecorate anytime I want without all the fuss."

Tim went back upstairs and found the guest room. He kicked off his sneakers, tossed his glasses onto the side table, and crawled into bed in the peaceful blue room. He stretched out and was asleep without even pulling down the window shades. He fell into a deep and blissfully dreamless sleep.

Chapter Six

TIM WOKE WITH A START.

"Where am I?" He sat up and peered around the dark room. His heart pounded. "How did I get here?" His hands fumbled and found a lamp. He switched it on and grabbed his glasses from the bedside table. His breathing gradually returned to normal. All those plants; the stars painted on the ceiling, the good smells coming up from downstairs. He lay back down, his arms behind his head. *Right. I'm in Zatanna's guest room. And soon, I'll be going with her to a supercool party.*

There was a sharp knock on the door. "Tim?" Zatanna called. "Are you up?"

"Yeah." Tim swung his legs over the side of the bed and reached for his shoes. He was still a little groggy.

"Well, come on down for dinner, and then we'll be off."

When Tim arrived in the kitchen, Yo-yo sat perched on a chair at the table, just like a member of the family. Zatanna was placing napkins beside the two plates. A casserole steamed in the center of the table.

"Vegetarian?" Tim asked.

"You bet," Zatanna said. "Veggie lasagna. Smells good, doesn't it?"

Tim nodded and sat down at the place mat that had a big glass of milk sitting on it. The other one had a glass of wine. Tim didn't need magic to know which was intended for him.

Zatanna sat opposite him and held up her glass. "To new friends," she toasted. Tim clinked her wineglass with his milk glass. He took a swig—and gagged.

"Oh dear," Zatanna said. "I guess you're not ready for soy milk yet." She crossed to the fridge and brought over a can of ginger ale. "How's this instead?"

Tim flipped open the soda and took a huge gulp. He swallowed. "Better!" he said.

"I guess the vegetarian thing needs to be introduced more gradually," Zatanna said with a grin. "Kind of like my mission to get Constantine to quit smoking!"

She served the lasagna and Tim scarfed it down. "Not all vegetarian stuff is awful," he admitted. "This is good!"

"Glad you like it."

Tim had seconds of the lasagna, and did the washing up while Zatanna changed for the party. Yo-yo helped straighten up by using his talons, bringing the place mats to the sideboard and dropping the paper napkins into the garbage. Once they were done, they went into the living room to wait for Zatanna.

"Ta-da!" Zatanna posed on the stairs. "How do I look?"

Tim's eyes nearly bugged out. The gorgeous magician wore a skimpy little outfit—the least amount of clothes Tim had ever seen on a girl up close. She looked very different in it than in the sweatshirt and leggings she had worn all day. Then he realized—the shiny top hat, spangly leotard, and black fishnet tights were exactly what she'd worn on TV.

"Is that your magic outfit?" Tim asked.

"My professional attire, yes." She came down the stairs, crossed to Tim, and pulled candy from his ear. She handed it to him with a grin. "It's kind of silly, but it's effective. And what's expected."

Tim laughed. "I like this kind of magic." He popped the candy into his mouth.

Zatanna shrugged. "A girl has to earn a living. So I'm a stage magician. Besides, it's a great way to keep my true identity hidden. By hiding in plain sight."

Tim heard a car honk outside. Zatanna pulled aside the curtain and peered out. "The taxi is here," she announced. She tapped her top hat and headed for the door. Tim and Yo-yo followed. Tim hesitated. *Should I be wearing a costume?* he wondered. As Yo-yo settled onto his shoulder, he decided that the bird could be his costume.

Zatanna smiled at him. "Even if John can't be here, we can still have fun, can't we?"

"Yeah! Sure we can," Tim assured her. He didn't want her to think he felt bad that John had left him with her. He really liked Zatanna.

"Good." She opened the door and stepped out into the balmy night.

"Uh, listen," Tim said. "If it's a rude question, you can tell me to mind my own business. But you and John Constantine . . . are you, um . . ." He didn't quite know how to ask.

Zatanna bailed him out. "Not anymore. Not really." She sighed. "I don't think he's the type for any kind of permanent relationship. If you know what I mean."

Tim nodded. "Yeah, he hasn't struck me as a particularly permanent person, so far. More like . . . an adventurer."

"Precisely. He's too much of a risk-taker—a gambler."

Her phrase startled Tim. That was exactly what Madame Xanadu's cards had said.

Zatanna paused and turned to face her house. "EsuoH, tcetorp flesruoy!" she declared.

Huh? Tim stared at her. "What did you say?" he asked.

"I told the house to protect itself," Zatanna explained. She tapped her top hat again and continued toward the taxi. "In case anyone tries to break in."

"It sounded like you were talking backward." Tim glanced back at the pink house. It didn't look any different. Was there really a spell on it?

"It's how I work the art. Verbally. I talk backward. It's more a concentration aid than anything else. My father used to do it, and I suppose I got the idea from him."

Tim remembered from Zatanna's TV interview that her father had also been a famous illusionist. He assumed magic would be easier if you grew up with it, inherited it through your bloodlines. You'd be more used to it. Tim wished his father could show him the ropes, gradually, instead of one whammy after another from all these strangers. But there was no way his father would believe in magic—let alone practice or teach it.

Zatanna opened the back door of the cab. Yo-yo flew inside.

"Hey!" the driver exclaimed. "Is the bird coming too?"

"Of course," Zatanna said, sliding into the cab. "It's Halloween."

The driver shook his head good-naturedly, as if he'd seen and heard it all before. "No problem. Happy Halloween."

Tim scrambled in beside Zatanna, and Yo-yo sat on his lap.

"We're going to a bar called Bewitched," Zatanna told the driver. "On Haight and Fillmore. Do you know it?"

The driver gave them a curious look in the rearview mirror. "Yeah. Never had anyone go there before."

As they drove through the twisting and hilly San Francisco streets, Tim gazed out the windows. Little kids in costumes held their parents' hands; kids his own age were dressed up too. He even saw adults wearing masks and elaborate makeup. Everyone seemed to be having fun.

"We don't have Halloween in England," he said to Zatanna. "Not like you do here. That's what I always thought of as magic. Ghosts and ghouls and witches and werewolves. It's like Constantine said. If you can imagine it, it's here in

America somewhere."

They pulled onto a dark street. Zatanna paid the driver as Tim and Yo-yo got out of the cab. Tim scanned the street; it was packed with cars and limos parked every which way. "Must be seriously rocking," he said. "Look at the crowd!"

Zatanna nodded and grinned. "Glad we didn't have to find a parking spot. I'd really need some magic tricks for that!"

They walked up to the club entrance. All the other buildings looked like abandoned warehouses. Tim suspected that had probably been the club's previous life as well. But now the word BEWITCHED glowed in a deep purple neon over the door, and even from outside in the street Tim could feel a pulsing bass line and drumbeat. He wished Molly could see him now. It would have been so cool if he could have brought her here. Actually, he wished all the kids who picked on him in London could see him too. *None of* them *would be able to get into this place*, he thought with pride.

At least, I think *I can get in*, Tim mused as he gazed up at the doorman's disdainful sneer.

"Sorry, kid, you can't come in here," the man said. He looked at Tim as if he were something to clean off a shoe. "Get lost. And take that stuffed bird with you." The man flicked his fingers at Tim and Yo-yo, brushing them off.

"Yo-yo's not stuffed," Tim replied indignantly. The owl fluffed his feathers as if he'd been insulted. "He's as real as you are!"

"Very funny. Isn't it after your bedtime?"

Zatanna stepped out of the shadows and into the light streaming out of the open door. "He's with me, Apollonius. So's the owl."

The man's face completely changed. So did his manner. "Why, Miss Zatanna," he gushed, "this *is* a welcome surprise. Please, go in. I'm sorry, child. Had I known you were with the enchantress . . ."

"Yeah, whatever." Tim smirked at the man. "That's what you get for being such a snob."

"I'm sure you're right, sir."

They stepped through the door and into a packed nightclub. Tim stared at the spectacle in front of him.

The dance floor was a few steps down from the entryway. Hundreds of people milled about, some dancing, some talking in groups, some observing, some arguing. Black and orange balloons perfect for the Halloween theme floated near the ceiling. Amber light and pink and gold fog piped in from the corners took all the hard edges off everything. Most of the men were in tuxedos, the women in fancy gowns. Hair was slicked back, piled high, decorated with jewels, multicolored, or nonexistent. Faces were grotesque, gorgeous, inhuman, animated. They were amazing exotic creatures, far from the inhabitants of Ravenknoll Estates, East London.

What struck Tim most was the energy that emanated from the sunken area—he could practically see sparks shooting between people, currents entwining them, clouds of excited air rising and swirling through the club. It surged up inside him, making him want to join in, swallow it whole, let it take him over completely.

Zatanna seemed to feel the excitement too. She was laughing. "I haven't come here for years. Makes me feel young again."

Startled, Tim stared at her. "You don't look old."

She gave him a little bow. "Thank you, young man. For that you deserve a drink."

As if summoned by Zatanna's words, a waitress appeared at Tim's side. "Can I take your order?

"Hello, Tala," Zatanna greeted the woman holding the tray. Tim couldn't help staring at her. She looked like a pretty and sophisticated woman in her thirties—except for her eyes. They were red-rimmed, with red pupils.

"Zatanna!" Tala exclaimed. "Nobody told me you were here!"

"This is my friend Timothy, Tal. Tala, Timothy. Tala's a queen of evil. She's an old acquaintance of the Trenchcoat Brigade."

Evil? Zatanna hangs out with evil magicians? And how would the Trenchcoat Brigade know her? Unless maybe they've been trying to catch her . . . ?

"Hi, Tim," Tala said, directing those red orbs at him. "Listen, we're getting kind of busy now. But I'll be back to talk later, when I'm on a break. Can I take your order?"

"Ice water for me," Zatanna said. "Tim?"

"Can I have a beer?" He figured, if she were a queen of evil, she shouldn't mind some underage drinking.

No such luck. "Only if you can show me a genuine ID proving you're over twenty-one."

Tim ducked his head sheepishly, and shoved his hands in his pockets.

Zatanna and Tala laughed. "Ginger ale?" Tala suggested.

"I suppose."

Tim watched as Tala disappeared into the gyrating crowd. "If she's a queen of evil," he asked, "why's she working here?"

"She's just resting between engagements, if you see what I mean."

Tim shook his head. He didn't see what she meant at all.

Zatanna clutched his arm. "Come on," she said. "There's someone here I want you to meet."

Zatanna led Tim around a group of very tall, thick men who were speaking with a group of very tiny thin men. She brought him over to the bar, where a slim man in a white tuxedo stood watching the party. He was quite pale, nearly as pale as his suit, and had very dark hair. He seemed pointy: his goatee pointy, his black eyebrows pointy, even his hair seemed to stand up in two little points on top of his head, as if he had horns. Something about him made Tim uneasy. Still, if Zatanna wanted him to meet the guy, he figured it would be okay.

"Tannarak—this young man is called Tim Hunter," Zatanna said. "Tannarak is another of the bad guys. He also owns this club."

The man's bloodred lips parted in a sinister smile. Did Zatanna actually like him? He gave Tim the creeps.

"Delightful as usual, Zatanna." He faced Tim. His eyes were also red-rimmed, like Tala's, Tim noted. "Charmed to make your acquaintance, young man. Now, Zatanna, I must take exception. I do not consider myself a 'bad guy.'"

Zatanna smiled. "Let's just say that we are usually on opposite sides of any . . . debate. It's Halloween. We can leave it at that."

"What does Halloween have to do with any-thing?" Tim asked.

"It is said that good and evil may come together on Halloween, if they choose, without ill effects," Tannarak explained. "Zatanna and I simply have different goals," he added. "But of course she is an honored guest here."

He tipped his head to Zatanna. She gave a tiny nod back. There seemed to be some agree-ment of respect between them, even if they might be enemies tomorrow.

"Now, young man. Is there anything you want to know?"

"Do you really do black magic?" Tim asked.

Tannarak sighed. "You see? We are much maligned by those in your circles, Zatanna. Already you are turning this young man's head." He poured himself a drink from an elegant blue bottle. A thin purple vapor rose up from the glass. He took a drink and then faced Tim. "There's no such thing as black magic. That's just a poor trans-lation. 'Necromancy' actually means 'Magic of the Dead,' but has roots in words meaning 'black.'"

"Like when kids play telephone?" Tim asked. "The final message is totally different from the original."

Tannarak gave Tim a look of admiration. "You have a fine pupil, Zatanna," he said. He ran a long, purple-tipped finger along his glass. "It's not 'black magic' versus 'white magic.' I tend to think of it as 'live magic' versus 'dead magic.'"

"Tannarak would like to live forever, so he's trying to find ways to defeat death," Zatanna explained. "And we sometimes disagree over methods," she added, with a hint of warning in her voice.

Tannarak ignored her. "But Tim, even that's too simplistic. Magic is about power."

With a move so sudden Tim barely detected it, Tannarak made the glass disappear. All that was left was the purple vapor. "It's the ability to see through the shadow to the real world beyond. And knowing what to do about it."

"I see. I think," Tim said. He cocked his head and narrowed his eyes. "And Tannarak isn't your real name, is it?"

A reptilian smile snaked across Tannarak's face again. "Names have power, child," he said, nodding. "You learn fast."

A small, bald man no taller than Tim's knees tugged at Tannarak's trouser leg. Tannarak glanced down. "Yes, Horatio?"

The small man didn't say a word, but Tannarak nodded a few times. He looked annoyed. "I told them to order twice as much woodbane for this crowd," he scolded. He looked at Tim and

Zatanna. "Can't find good help these days. Please excuse me. Hosting duties prevail."

Tannarak and Horatio vanished into the crowd, and Tim leaned against the bar, surveying the amazing scene before him. A woman floated by him, a few inches above the floor. An enormous, powerfully built man smiled at her, revealing two sets of pointed teeth. Three girls clustered nearby, changing colors as their argument heated up. From what Tim could hear, the blue one thought the red one had used a spell incorrectly. He did a double-take when he realized they were a set of Siamese triplets. A figure with a wolf's head nodded at Zatanna, who nodded slowly back. Tim could smell the foul odor of the creature's animal breath.

"I just realized something," Tim said. "The people here—none of them are wearing masks, are they?"

"That's right," Zatanna said. "In here, the masks are off. It's out there"—she waved toward the doorway—"that's where masks are worn."

"And they come and go like regular people?" Tim asked.

"Not exactly like regular people," Zatanna corrected. "But yes, there is interaction."

Tim let out a low whistle. "It's like there's a whole other world that I never knew existed, side by side with the real one."

Zatanna looked down into her glass of water. "Yes. And once you enter it, you can never leave." She looked up and gazed directly at Tim. Her blue eyes were intense, causing Tim to step back. Then what she'd said sunk in.

"Never?" he repeated.

Zatanna's expression softened. "You haven't entered it yet, Tim," she said. "You're a guest."

Tim nodded. Constantine had said he'd have to make a choice, that it's what this journey was all about. He had a feeling Zatanna was trying to make him understand how momentous—and irreversible—that decision was.

Tim looked back out at the party. Now that he'd been there for a while, he was beginning to see through the glamour and the excitement, the gorgeous lighting and good music. He was sensing something else—an undercurrent he couldn't identify. Whatever it was, it made him uncomfortable. It was the way he felt when he had to walk past the abandoned lot on the corner of Gladstone and Pine; the bullies weren't necessarily going to jump him each time, but he was braced for it anyway. Even when they weren't there, the lot seemed filled with their antagonism.

Yo-yo was fidgeting on Tim's shoulder. Maybe the bird was picking up something too.

Tim looked over at Zatanna. If she was cool, then he was just being paranoid, and Yo-yo was responding to his jitters. After all, she was the real magician here; these were her friends, this was her scene.

Uh-oh. Lines of worry creased Zatanna's smooth, pale forehead.

"Zatanna?" he said. "Is something wrong?"

"I'm starting to think there might very well be," she answered. She scanned the crowd. "There isn't a single practitioner here who doesn't work the dark side."

"And that's . . . unusual?" Tim asked. He didn't know how these magical Halloween parties worked.

Zatanna nodded slowly. "The Halloween truce usually brings out an even number of light and dark, good and bad. In fact, it's that balance that ensures the pact isn't broken. That's how the truce is enforced."

"You're saying you're the only good guy here?" Tim asked. *This is not good*, he thought. In fact, he'd go so far as to say that it was seriously bad.

"I think the invitation may have been a trap," Zatanna admitted. She clenched her fist. "And I fell for it."

"What do we do now?" Tim asked.

"We get out of here—fast," Zatanna said.

"Act as if you're having the time of your life, but follow me to the door."

Plastering big smiles on their faces, Zatanna and Tim and Yo-yo began to weave their way through the crowd. Tim was sure the creatures near him could hear the loud thudding of his heart, smell the terror in the sweat that was beading up along his hairline.

A spotlight blasted on, catching Tim and Zatanna in its beam. They froze, trapped in its glare. A loudspeaker crackled. Tim turned back and saw that Tannarak had taken to the stage and stood in front of a standing microphone.

"Ladies and gentlemen and other entities," he boomed. "I have an announcement. It seems there's a special young lad in our audience tonight. Some of you may have already heard about him."

"Oh shoot," Zatanna said. "I'm sorry, Tim. I should never have brought you here." She took his hand and squeezed it. It didn't make Tim feel much better.

"As you know, there is a price on his head," Tannarak continued. "Which need not be attached to his body," he added with his snake-like smile.

Zatanna placed a hand on Tim's shoulder. "This boy is under my protection," she declared.

"Anyone who wishes to hurt him must first reckon with me."

Tannarak laughed. "My dear Zatanna, you are powerful, yes. But face facts. There's one of you and over a hundred of us. The kid is history."

Chapter Seven

TERROR SHOT THROUGH Tim, like nothing he had ever experienced before. He could *feel* the power emanating from these creatures.

He and Zatanna were surrounded on all sides. Creatures—human and nonhuman—circled in, closer and closer.

Tim squeezed his eyes shut. He couldn't bear to look into the grotesque and evil faces. Then the whispers began.

"Come to me, boy. I will give you the power to eat life."

"No! Give me your powers! I will reward you by allowing you to be my servant."

The whispers and murmurs were insistent, insinuating like smoke into his brain. Tim covered his ears, but he could still hear the summons of the practitioners, each trying to win his powers, to take him over, and failing that, to kill him.

"Kcab ffo!" Zatanna shouted. "Teg yawa!"

Tim sensed a gap between him and whoever had been in front of him. Zatanna must have pushed them away with her backward speaking.

The murmurs continued, but now they addressed Zatanna as well. "I am the Queen of Mirrors! Woman, give me the boy or one night your reflection will sneak out of its frame and cut your sleeping throat!"

"If you stand in our way we will feed the boy your heart before we cut his own out to increase our power!"

Smells came to Tim: sulfur, lizards, mud. Something flicked the side of his face and his eyes popped open. Tentacles reached for him over Zatanna's shoulder. A clawed hand had its talons in Zatanna's long hair. Tim felt nauseous from the fear. *We're done for*, he thought.

Then—"Constantine!" a shocked voice called out.

Tim whirled around. Slouched in the doorway, John Constantine lit one of his ever-present cigarettes.

"Nobody touches the boy," he said.

All murmurs, all movement, stopped. Time seemed suspended in the dead silence. Constantine took a step into the room.

"That's right. The boy's mine. And in thirty

seconds me and him, and the witch, are going to walk out of here. Oh, yeah," he added. "The owl too." He surveyed the room for a moment. "You know who I am. My reputation. Or you ought to. Now . . ." He paused to take a deep drag from the cigarette. "Does anyone here really want to start something?"

Tim held his breath. Zatanna's grip on his arm tightened. No one moved. No one spoke.

"Right," Constantine said to Tim and Zatanna. "Come on, you lot. We're leaving."

Tim didn't need to be told twice. He beat it out of there fast—so fast he was outside and breathing hard before Zatanna and John had left the building. He leaned against the wall and took in great gulps of night air.

Tim wondered what would have happened if John hadn't shown up. What kind of magic would they have performed on him? Would he be dead now? Or perhaps death would have been a better alternative to what those creatures had in mind. What was he mixed up in?

And yet . . . shot through Tim's fears was the glimmering knowledge that he was somehow important. Important enough to kill. To fight over. To defend. It was a heady feeling.

The door to the club slammed. "I could have stopped them, you know," Zatanna complained.

"Yeah, you probably could." John sounded amused.

Zatanna, on the other hand, sounded exasperated. "John, you don't have any power to speak of. Any one of them could have torn you to shreds. But they—they were scared of you." Her wide eyes searched his face for answers. Answers Tim didn't think she'd get. He knew that much about Constantine by now. "I don't understand what happened back there."

"Magic."

She folded her arms over her chest. "Seriously, John."

"A good magician never reveals his secrets, love. *You* taught me that. But it helps that they're all a few guppies short of an aquarium."

"Speak English, can't you?"

"I speak perfect English," John protested. "So does Tim. It's you that's got the funny accent."

John gave Tim a wink.

Tim laughed and Zatanna shook her head. Then she touched a hand to John's cheek and turned his face to the streetlight. Tim could see a dark bruise under John's eye, and what looked like burns along his jaw.

"What happened to your face?" Zatanna asked. "What happened in Calcutta?"

"The usual." John shrugged her away.

"Mr. Constantine." Now Zatanna sounded like a kindergarten teacher reprimanding a small child. "Are you mysterious about everything?"

"Who, me? Transparent as glass, I am."

An expression came over Zatanna's face that Tim had seen frequently on Molly. She wasn't backing down. "It would be a lot easier to protect Tim if he and I both knew what was threatening him."

"Yeah," Tim seconded. "I have a right to know. I mean, it's all about me, isn't it?"

John gave them a weary look and ran a hand through his blond hair. "All right, all right. Calcutta is a stronghold of the Cold Flame. It's where they've been putting up, lately. We wanted to take them out—weaken their numbers. So we did."

"But why are they after me?" Tim asked. "I'm not the one who can do magic."

"Not yet. They don't want you to live up to your full potential," John explained.

Tim snorted. "My teachers at school already say that I'm not. Living up to my full potential, I mean."

"Well, the Cold Flame don't want you to live—at all," John said grimly. "Because if you develop in the way that you could, you might become a great threat."

"There's more to it, isn't there?" Zatanna asked.

"Not yet," John said. "Right now their goals are clear. They may shift."

"What do you mean?" Tim demanded.

"If they can't kill you, then they will try like Hades to win you over to their side," John said. "Which would put you and me on opposing teams."

"I would never do that!" Tim exploded. "How can you say that?"

Zatanna put a hand on Tim's shoulder. "It's all right, Tim. We both know how you feel." She looked at John. "Now that you're back, does that mean you and Tim will be leaving?"

John nodded. "Places to go, people to see. All that."

After all the recent excitement, Tim wasn't sure he wanted to have any new experiences. He felt that the ones he'd had so far would hold him for quite some time. Besides, he liked Zatanna and her cheerful sunny house, and he'd hoped she would teach him some magic tricks to show Molly before he had to leave.

Before he could protest, though, Zatanna turned and placed her hands on his shoulders.

"Tim, it was great meeting you," she said. "Call me the next time you're in the States, okay?"

Well, that ended that. Tim forced a smile. "Of course," he told her. "You've been terrific. Thanks for everything. Except the soy milk," he added with a grin.

Zatanna gave him a squeeze. "No problem. You were a great house guest. You and Yo-yo."

Yo-yo hovered in front of Zatanna and nodded his head as if to say good-bye.

Zatanna put her hands on her hips and crossed to Constantine. "Now, John Constantine. I don't think I'll ever understand you. Not if I live to be a thousand."

"No? And I'm such an uncomplicated bloke. You're slipping." They smiled at each other. "Give us a kiss and I'll be out of your life for another year or so."

Tim turned away as they kissed. He only turned back when he heard John speaking again.

"By the way," John said, "I almost forgot. We haven't got passports or tickets. Uh, could you, y'know, twitch your nose or something?"

Zatanna shook her head and laughed. "Jerk. You're practically useless. Stropssap dna stekcit raeppa."

Tim felt groggy, as if he were awakening from a deep sleep. Then he tried to sit bolt upright and felt himself restrained by a seat belt. *How'd that happen?* he wondered.

They were back aboard a plane, once again without seeming to travel there. Tim, who had never been outside of England in all his thirteen years, had now flown over the ocean to New York City, traveled across the huge United States to California, and was back on his second international flight. All within the space of what? A few days? His head swam.

"Okay, kiddo," John said, leaning back into his seat. "So what have you learned so far?"

"Learned?"

"Yeah. Come on. I've dragged you halfway around the world, you've been introduced to, insulted, or threatened by some of the most powerful practitioners of the art in existence. What have you learned?"

"I dunno. That all of them except Zatanna are about as well-balanced as upturned eggs." He could have made a point of including John Constantine in that group but decided against it.

"Yeah, that's a good beginning."

Tim thought more about what this trip had shown him, what was new information. "And that they don't live in the same world that most people do. Their world is like a shadow of ours. Dark and distorted, but still connected. At least with the bad guys. I guess with the good guys too. Like Zatanna. She's half in and half out of ordinary living." He twisted in his seat to gauge John's reaction. "Am I making sense?"

John looked thoughtful. "More than you know."

Tim sensed admiration in John's blue eyes and he smiled. It felt good to have earned this elusive, unpredictable fellow's respect.

Constantine reached for the headphones in the pocket of the seat in front of him. "Dr. Occult will be your guide for the next leg of the trip."

"Where's he going to take me, then? Tibet? Outer space?"

"Fairyland."

Tim stared at John, who fiddled with the headphones, calm as a quiet lake. Tim stared some more. Finally he managed to find his voice. But all that came out of his mouth was . . .

"Fairyland?"

Chapter Eight

IT HAD HAPPENED AGAIN. One minute Tim was squeezed into an airplane seat with a ginger ale on his tray table, and the next minute he was . . . where? He looked around. Some pretty, misty countryside that looked bucolic. Dr. Occult stood nearby, watching Yo-yo circling overhead.

He wished they'd quit doing that to him. This unconventional travel threw him off his game. Tim wondered if he had broken the sound barrier or the speed of light with all this hopping about. His molecules had to be scrambled by now.

Was this Fairyland? He scanned the land-scape. It just looked like a prettier part of England than he was used to. The large telegraph towers dotting the horizon confirmed that he was still in the so-called "real" world. Unless fairies communicated via telegraph or cable lines.

Constantine must have been kidding about
Fairyland, Tim decided. He was a joker, Tim
knew, even if he didn't always get the joke.

"Where's Constantine?" he asked.

"With the others," Dr. Occult answered.

"Which is where?" Tim asked.

"Not our concern, at the moment," Dr. Occult
answered. "Come, we are near our destination."

Tim followed Dr. Occult along a winding
country road. The damp day had left the path
soggy and muddy, and the grass smelled wet and
green. Nearby, a trickling stream meandered
through the hilly banks. Yo-yo's attention was
diverted by rabbits, or birds, or insects going
about their business and oblivious to the strange
trio journeying through their territory.

This isn't so bad, Tim thought, gazing around
at the peaceful greens of trees, shrubs, and grass.
If he could just get used to the shock of being
transported suddenly from one place to another,
he'd be fine. *Star Trek* had nothing on this! Tim's
shoulders dropped; he hadn't realized they'd been
hunched up near his ears. Fear still lurked inside
him, but he was finally relaxing into the adventure, starting to feel as if this could be his world,
his life. *Maybe I'm not crazy*, he thought, reaching for a tree branch and shaking down some

dew-flecked leaves. As whacked as it was, some-how this kind of living made more sense than things did back in London.

"So are you a real doctor?" Tim asked his companion.

"Am I a real doctor of what?"

Tim shrugged. "I don't know. What kind of things can you be a doctor of?"

"I'm not a medical doctor, if that's what you mean. Although I can set a bone or stanch the flow of blood if need be."

"Dr. Occult," Tim pronounced. He shook his head. "It's a funny name."

"Name?" Dr. Occult raised an eyebrow, but he was smiling, so Tim realized his error.

"Thing to be called, then," Tim corrected himself.

"We must wait here."

They were beside a large apple tree, each branch drooping under the weight of the bountiful fruit. A low fence separated the fields, and, all around them, as far as Tim could see, there was open pasture. Off in the distance he spotted woods, and beyond that, hills.

"Wait for what?" Tim asked. A fairy escort?

"For the sun to set. We must leave in twilight."

The sun was low on the horizon, so Tim

figured they didn't have too long a wait. Yo-yo settled onto a nearby branch. Tim plucked an apple that dangled in front of him.

He looked at Dr. Occult, feeling more at ease with him than he did with the others, despite Dr. Occult's formal attitude. Tim liked John the best, but he wasn't exactly a comforting presence. With John, he felt constantly on high alert; it was exciting but exhausting.

"Will you tell me something?" Tim asked.

"Possibly."

Tim snorted. *Never can get an easy yes or no from these guys.* He took a bite of the apple. "You four," he said, chewing. "Who are you? I mean, Constantine. He's just a bloke, isn't he?"

Dr. Occult gazed off into the distance, as if trying to decide how to answer—or whether to answer at all. "John Constantine," Dr. Occult said. "Yes. He has seen a great deal, and now he dances on the edge of the known like a crazy man. Because he is John Constantine, and because he is alive."

Tim took that in. Did these trenchcoat guys go to a special school to learn to speak in this high-handed, overly poetic way? "So you're saying it's just who he is, to be that way."

"Yes. It is his nature."

Tim chewed his apple thoughtfully. Dr. Occult at least was a little more forthcoming with answers, even if he had trouble understanding them. "How about Mister E? Is he really blind?"

"Oh yes. He is an extremist. He fights what he sees as the forces of darkness. That is his only purpose; it's what drives him. But sometimes I suspect that all he *can* see is darkness. However, he can travel in ways that even I cannot."

Tim remembered that Zatanna hadn't seemed too crazy about Mister E either. Maybe none of them liked the guy, but he had some skills, so they put up with him. Like choosing Bobby Saunders for football. He was a pain, but boy, he could kick. And more important, you didn't want him playing for the *other* team.

"And the other one?" Tim asked. "He spooks me. He seems really . . . different."

"The Stranger? Ahh . . . I have encountered him many times in the past." Dr. Occult slipped his hands into the pockets of his trench coat and nodded. It was hard for Tim to make out his face under the brimmed hat. "He walks his own path. One that began too long ago, and I suspect has no end in sight. I do not know his story. I know no one who does. Perhaps he has walked for such a long time that he himself no longer remembers."

How could someone forget who he is? Tim decided not to bother asking and skipped to his next question. "And what about you?" he asked. Would Dr. Occult be as open about himself as he'd been about the others?

"I am your guide through this stage of your journey, Timothy Hunter. And you may trust me. Empty your pockets."

So that's that. Interview over. Oh well, I did the best I could.

Tim tossed away the apple core, rummaged through his pockets, and pulled out the contents. String, a stubby pencil, two markers, keys, coins, gum, lint. A trading card.

Dr. Occult peered at the objects in his hands. "Leave the keys and the coins here," he instructed. "Cold iron will not be welcome where we go. The rest you may retain."

Tim looked around. "Where should I . . . ?" He didn't want to lose his stuff. "Got it!" Kneeling by a large tree root, he dug a little hole and put his coins and keys into it. He patted the dirt over the top.

"Hope I can remember where I put them," he said, standing back up again. He knocked the dirt from the knees of his jeans.

"Listen to me carefully now," Dr. Occult said.

"There are things you must remember. You must obey my orders explicitly and in all things, no matter how petty or strange they seem to you."

"Oookay," Tim agreed. He didn't like just accepting terms without knowing what they were. What if Dr. Occult told him to jump off Tower Bridge? Would he do it? That's what Molly always asked. But it wasn't as if he had much choice. And Dr. Occult knew a lot more about where they were going than he did.

"Secondly," Dr. Occult continued, "ask no questions or favors of those you meet on our travels. Accept no gifts or foodstuff without my permission."

Tim nodded. *Keep your mouth shut*, he translated for himself, *and no goodies*. He sighed. That meant no souvenirs. Too bad. He would have loved to pick up some kind of magic toy for Molly.

"Thirdly, remember your manners. Etiquette will be important where we go, and good manners are gold. For a trivial impoliteness you could find yourself cursed with donkey's ears, or worse. And lastly, *never* stray from the path. No matter what you see, or hear, or feel." Dr. Occult studied Tim seriously, gazing deep into his eyes, as if he could burrow into his mind to make sure the rules stuck. "Do you understand?"

Tim wiped his hands on his shirt. His palms

had grown sweaty while he listened to Dr. Occult's instructions. "I suppose." He had been feeling more comfortable with all this magic stuff—until he was bombarded with all these rules! *Everything with magic is so complicated*, he thought. *So filled with consequence.*

Dr. Occult nodded. "Good." He gazed up at the sky. Streaks of purple and pink dyed the clouds, and the sun hung fat and heavy in the treetops. The sky above was deepening to indigo. Mist rose as twilight spread across the quiet countryside.

"We are ready to begin our journey. Wait here," Dr. Occult said, and he pointed to a small gate that stood alone in the distance. "I will walk across to that wicket gate. When I wave to you, then walk as I walked, along that path. When you cross the stream, take care not to get your feet wet. Yes?"

"Fine." Tim nodded. This whole thing seemed bizarre to him. He watched Dr. Occult make his way down the hill, toward the stream and then to the gate, which Tim hadn't noticed before. In fact, he was pretty sure there had been nothing on that side of the stream until the sun had gone down. But other than the gate, all he could see there was more of the same pretty countryside. Nothing special. Why there would be a lone wooden gate, unconnected to any fence, he couldn't imagine.

As he watched Dr. Occult cross the stream, Tim's heart started to thump. Would he remember all the rules? Were they really going to Fairyland? And would he make it back out again—that was the bigger, underlying worry, too big to even think about. Tim shook off the idea before it could settle into his brain and scramble it.

He heard Yo-yo's flapping wings above him, and was glad to have the bird along as company. "Yo-yo, why are we doing this?" He looked up at the bird. "I guess you're kind of along for the ride. Where I go you go, right?"

The bird circled his head.

"Okay, then, why am *I* doing this? Anyone with half an ounce of sense would have told them all to bugger off at the beginning."

Dr. Occult gave the signal, a short wave, without turning to face Tim.

"Oh, well," Tim said. "Too late to back out now." He looked up at the bird and shrugged. "No one's ever accused me of having any sense anyway."

Tim hurried along the path Dr. Occult had taken. Not wanting to make any mistakes, he even went so far as to put his feet into Dr. Occult's large and muddy footprints. He made it down to the stream.

"Here goes." He carefully crossed the little stream, glad that his shoes had rubber soles to help him grip the slippery rocks. *Don't get your feet wet*, he reminded himself. *I suppose they don't have door mats where we're going, and they don't want us to track in mud*.

Tim came up behind Dr. Occult, who still hadn't moved. His hand was on the gate. Yo-yo landed on one of its posts.

"I'm here. Uh . . . Doctor?"

"Yes?"

"Constantine said we were going to Fairyland. He was kidding, wasn't he?"

"We travel through the Fair Lands, child. Call them Avalon, or Elvenhome, or Faerie. It matters not. It is the land of Summer's Twilight."

"Oh." Tim wasn't sure if he felt better or worse—or just weirder. "So when do we go there?"

"Look behind you."

Tim's heart pounded as he slowly turned around to face the way they had come.

The landscape had changed. The apple tree, the cable wires, the path, the stream—all had vanished. He gazed at a glittering sunrise over a crystal-clear lake, only the purples and pinks were paler than he'd seen in any sunrise, softer and all-encompassing.

"We have already left your world," Dr. Occult said. "This wooden gate exists in both worlds— here and there."

"You mean, people can just cross over like that?" Tim asked.

"There are many places common to more than one plane," Dr. Occult explained. "They are accessible to those who know the path to walk."

"Um, I see. I think. Where do we go now?"

"Through the gate. And once through it, you may notice a few changes."

Tim gulped. More changes? Could he take any more? "Like what?"

"You'll see."

Dr. Occult swung open the little wooden gate. Together he and Tim walked through it. When they came out the other side, Tim stared at Dr. Occult. He had turned into a *she*!

"Dr. Occult?" Tim gaped at the woman standing beside him. She was tall, with short, straight brown hair. Her angular face was pretty but plain. She wore no makeup, and her clothes were simple—a jacket, a blouse, a skirt. She would have looked at home in an office, rather than a magical kingdom. "Is that what you really look like?"

"No. I am no longer Dr. Occult, although we share certain purposes in common. He is himself as I am me, but I am still your guide."

"I don't understand." Tim couldn't stop staring, even though he knew it was rude and that he'd been warned to have good manners in this place.

"Dr. Occult and I represent different aspects of a single entity. Male and female. Anima and animus."

Like in the cards that Madame X had read, Tim realized. A man in touch with his feminine side. Here was Dr. Occult's feminine side—in the flesh. What else had that card predicted? Oh yeah. That it could represent several women connected to his safety and identity. Zatanna was probably part of that card too.

"These are things we all carry within ourselves. In this world, I prefer to highlight the female."

"What's your—" Tim was about to ask the woman, who used to be Dr. Occult, what her name was, but then he remembered the rules. "I mean, please, what are you called?"

"Find a name for me," the woman challenged.

"Find one?" Tim asked.

"That's right."

"A name? Yours?" Tim was confused.

"It's a test, of sorts," the woman said.

"I bet it's bloody Rumpelstiltskin," Tim muttered under his breath. They strolled in silence for a little while. *How am I supposed to guess her name? Or make one up for her?* His eye was drawn to a rosebush by the side of the path. They were enormous, beautiful, and the scent wafted their way, filling Tim with a sudden inspiration. He faced the woman. "Rose," he announced. "I'll call you Rose."

The woman looked startled, then smiled. "That's good, Tim. And fast. The Stranger was right. You have the potential for power."

Tim was pleased that he'd passed this first round, yet didn't understand what the big deal was about giving her a name. Or maybe, rather than giving her a name, he had *guessed* it.

"So we're there?" Tim asked, looking around.

"We have arrived in the realm of Faerie, yes."

Dr. Occult, now Rose, led Tim and Yo-yo through a beautiful wooded area. The dirt path was soft under Tim's feet, and the trees glistened in the sunlight—brighter even than Zatanna's living room in California. Flowers that Tim had never seen before dotted the road. Every now and then he spotted colorful creatures flitting in and out of leaves and bushes. Birds? He wondered. No, their movements were too quick. Butterflies, maybe. But butterflies didn't giggle, and he was certain he heard the tinkling sound of something tiny laughing.

He took a deep breath, filling his lungs with the scent of flowers, of hopes, of possibilities. *If wishing has a smell*, Tim thought, *this is it*.

Yo-yo flew overhead, his yellow eyes darting about, taking in every stray movement in the foliage around them. To Tim, the bird seemed happy, alert, more . . . *itself* somehow. Maybe because Yo-yo was made of magic, he reasoned, Faerie seemed more like home.

"So where are we off to?" Tim asked. He wondered if Dr. Occult—Rose—had a destination in mind, or if they were just setting off to see what adventure would jump out and snatch them. Right now, Tim felt game for anything. He liked what he'd seen of Faerie so far. It was true that all he had seen so far was pretty landscape, but there was a feeling here that made his chest expand, made his limbs swing. It was the giddiness of anticipation.

Rose pulled aside some low branches and gestured for Tim to step through.

"What are we going to do now?" he asked.

"We are going to market!" Rose replied.

Tim ducked down and stepped between the shrubs. He came out at the edge of a meadow—a meadow filled with amazing sights, sounds, and smells.

Colorful booths dotted the grass, and creatures of all description strolled among them. Tables strewn with goods, elves wearing sandwich boards advertising wares, and goblins carrying trays filled with strange objects all competed for attention. Rough wood picnic tables were set up, and a large roasting pit emitted great puffs of delicious-smelling smoke. Serving maids—with delicate transparent wings—darted between customers, filling and refilling glasses with colorful liquids.

"Awesome!" Tim tried to look everywhere at once, until he realized that would only give him a headache. Everywhere he turned there was a vision out of a fairy tale, an illustration from a fantasy book!

"'Ere, you! Young feller-me-lad! Come 'ere!"

Tim looked to see who had called to him. He spotted a booth where a strange creature, with skin the color of a wheat stalk and just as fuzzy, waved a skinny, long-fingered hand. Tim figured there'd be no harm in checking out the creature's wares. He knew not to buy anything. He'd just window-shop, or rather, counter-shop.

Tim stepped over to the booth. Yo-yo fluttered down and perched on his shoulder. He patted the bird's talons, smiling. Yo-yo wanted to window-shop too.

Now that Tim was closer, he could see that the creature was much smaller than he had realized—just four feet high. Its pointed ears poked through wispy silver hair.

"I'll swap you your heart's desire fer a year of yer life."

Tim stared at the creature. It must be kidding. How could it be offering to sell someone his heart's desire?

"No?" The creature stroked its stubbly cheeks. "I'll trade for yer voice, then. Or the color of yer eyes."

Tim had to force himself not to laugh. It seemed so . . . so . . . ludicrous. Fantastic. Bizarre. How could he possibly give away the blue of his eyes? And why would anyone want it? Who knew there was a market for such things?

Tim remembered Dr. Occult's instructions, before he had turned into Rose: manners mattered.

"No, thank you," he said politely. "But thanks for thinking of me."

But the creature wouldn't quit. "One of your fingers, then. You've got ten of the little buggers." He waved a hand at Tim, and Tim realized the

Faerie creature only had four fingers on its hand. "You'll never miss one. It's yer heart's desire I'm offerin', ducky. None of yer tat." The creature sighed as if it was about to make a huge sacrifice. "All right," it grumbled. "Two toes. And six months of yer old age for your heart's desire. And that's me final offer."

"No, thanks," Tim said. "But thank you, anyway."

Rose stepped up to join them. The creature ignored her and continued to talk to Tim. "I can tell you've come a long way, dearie. Here. Let me give you a flask of my best berryjuice for yer journey."

Rose spoke before Tim could respond. "We must thank you for the offer, mistress, but also decline it."

So the creature was female. It was hard for Tim to tell.

"The boy is under my protection," Rose explained. "We cannot dally amongst the Fair Folk."

"Fair spoken," said the creature. "I wish you good traveling, and that's for free."

"Hey!" Tim cried out as Yo-yo made a sharp sudden movement. He fluttered off Tim's shoulder, swerved, and swooped behind Tim.

"Ger off!" shouted a small creature kneeling behind Tim. Yo-yo dug his talons into the creature's hand—a hand that was reaching for Tim's pocket.

"What's going on?" Rose asked.

The creature froze, then fell over. "This bird of yours attacked me! I demand compensation!"

Chapter Nine

TIM STARED DOWN AT the little creature who lay moaning in agony on the ground.

The creature sniveled and groaned, clutching its hand. Tim had no idea what kind of critter it was—it didn't look like pictures he'd seen of elves or fairies, and it certainly didn't look like the garden gnomes in his neighbor's dismal yard. It was small and wiry, covered in yellowish fur. It wore only a leather vest and short medieval-looking knickers. But what most tripped Tim up in identifying the creature was its long tail thrashing along the ground, kicking up dirt. A bracelet lay in the dirt nearby.

"Ooooooh," the creature moaned. "That is a terrible, dangerous beast. Attacking me without warning! It shouldn't roam free!"

"Yo-yo," Rose said, addressing the owl. "Is this true?"

"Whoo!" Yo-yo responded, flying to Rose's outstretched fingers.

"Is that so?" Rose said to Yo-yo. Tim stared at them. Could Rose actually understand what Yo-yo was saying?

Rose turned to the little creature. "The owl tells me that you were trying to put that bracelet into Timothy's pocket. The bird saw you, and stopped you."

Tim frowned in confusion. Why would the little creature put a bracelet *into* his pocket? What would it gain? Pickpockets usually took things *out* of people's pockets—not put them in. It didn't make sense.

"Rubbish!" the creature protested. "It was an unprovoked attack!" It scrambled up into a crouch, tucking its tail around itself. It grabbed the bracelet and shoved it onto its skinny arm. "But I have thought better of demanding compensation, and will be content to let the matter rest here."

"You may be," Rose countered, "but I am not. Where is the warden of the market?"

The creature rubbed its hands together over and over. "Oh, don't bother Old Glory with this," it said, its voice oozy. "Glory hates to be bothered with market affairs."

"Market affairs *are* Glory's business, Snout."

A bespectacled man stepped through the crowd. He was dressed in mismatching old-fashioned clothes: a long blue velvet jacket over purple velvet trousers, a ruffled white shirt with a bow tie, a green velvet vest, and shoes that buttoned up the sides. His gray hair was thick, as were the gray muttonchop sideburns that covered half his face. But other than the slight point to his ears, the man looked pretty much human to Tim. Much more so than little Snout, whose tail was thrashing again.

"As warden, market traders are my affairs as well," Glory continued. He glared down at Snout, who sat at the man's feet, wringing his hands.

Glory crossed his arms over his chest. "Here is what I see," he surmised. "You would have planted the bracelet in the child's pocket, waited until he was about to leave the market, then shouted 'Stop, thief!'"

So that *had been Snout's plan*, Tim thought. The scheme made some sense. In the strange worlds he was visiting, anything was possible. Tim suspected that logic as he knew it was gone forever.

Glory went on detailing what he believed to have been Snout's con game. "And as the wronged party, you would have been entitled to keep the boy as your personal servant for seventy years.

And to claim restitution from his companions into the bargain."

Tim gulped. They took stealing really seriously here. He was relieved that the warden knew he hadn't stolen the jewelry. Dr. Occult—Rose—was right. He had to stay on his toes and follow the rules in this place.

Snout wriggled his way up to standing, tugging on Glory's trousers to do so. "Er, Lord Glory—"

"Silence!" Glory waved a hand.

Tim's eyes widened in shock. Snout's mouth vanished! Clearly, Glory didn't kid around when he wanted someone to shut up. Tim knew he'd remember that bit of information as well.

Glory bent down so he could grip Snout's shoulder, as if he suspected the creature would run away. "I regret that Snout's action has tarnished the name of the market," he said to Tim. "You may claim restitution."

Tim almost felt sorry for Snout, until he remembered that he had narrowly missed being the creature's servant for the next seventy years.

"Lead us to your barrow," Glory ordered Snout.

Tim felt as if all eyes were on them as they left the market. They followed a narrow path into the woods and soon arrived at a small hill. Snout brushed aside leaves and shrubs, revealing a small wooden door. He pulled a key out of a vest pocket, inserted it, and opened the door into the hillside.

Tim, Rose, and Glory all had to crouch in order to step through the little door. It was a tight fit inside. The place was filled with junk: broken furniture, boxes, crates, chests, odds and ends. A little stove, table, and chair were set in one corner, and a bed was dug into the dirt wall, like a bunk. The rest was just . . . stuff.

"Now then, Snout," ordered Glory. "You have wronged this boy and the owl. As market warden, here is my judgment. Each may take, for free and without obligation, one item from your barrow."

Tim looked up at Rose. "Can I?" he asked. He wanted to be sure he was allowed to do this. He had already learned that there were surprising consequences in Faerie.

"Yes," she replied.

Yo-yo fluttered to a coatrack standing haphazardly at an angle by the door. Several necklaces and scarves dangled from it. The owl caught up a silvery chain in his talons and flew to Lord Glory.

Lord Glory nodded, as if giving the bird permission. "Of course," he said to Yo-yo. "If that is what you want." He turned to Tim. "Now you, mortal child."

Tim didn't know what to take. The room was

stuffed with oddities. He could have spent days here, exploring, examining, finding out what everything was, how it worked. But he knew he shouldn't dawdle.

He stepped carefully deeper into the crowded barrow, trying to not knock anything over. He noticed a fancy-looking book, but didn't pick it up. A shining sphere rotating slowly on a brass stand caught his eye, but he decided against it. He spotted a weird little gnome statue that might make Molly laugh. As he reached over a table to take it, his hand tingled. Startled, Tim dropped his arm to his side. He reached again, and the same thing happened, just as his fingers passed over a sturdy little teapot.

Funny, he thought. *It's as if the teapot is trying to tell me something*. He lifted the teapot from its spot. It was a lot heavier than it looked. Opening it, Tim discovered why.

Inside, there was a glowing egg. Tim lifted it out. "Can I have this?" he asked.

"A Mundane Egg," Lord Glory said, surprised. "Well, well. Who'd have thought that our Snout would have such a thing? And hidden amongst trinkets."

"Hidden in plain sight?" Tim ventured, remembering the phrase of Zatanna's.

"Could say so. You chose well, boy. Luck—or

something similar—is on your side." Lord Glory stroked his fluffy sideburns. "A Mundane Egg. Who'd have thought it? When I return your mouth to you, Snout, we must discuss this at length."

Rose carefully wrapped the necklace chain around Yo-yo's neck. "We will leave this place now, Lord Glory," she said. "With your permission."

"Of course, my lady. Good-bye. And good-bye, child. Guard the egg."

"'Bye," Tim replied. He glanced down at the egg in his hand. It was shinier and heavier than the kind he scrambled at home, but he couldn't see why Lord Glory was making such a fuss over it. And didn't "mundane" mean ordinary? Still, he took care when he placed it in his pocket. After all, an egg was an egg, mundane or not. He didn't want to smash it in his jeans and wind up drippy with yolk.

They left Snout's barrow. Rose, Tim, and Yo-yo continued along the path.

"I'm hungry," Tim said. "Is there anything to eat?"

"No," Rose replied. "You mustn't eat anything in Faerie, Tim. Not if you want to get back. Or at least, get back to the time that you left. A day in Faerie can be a hundred years in mortal lands."

"So I stay hungry?"

"You get even hungrier."

That didn't sound promising. "So where are we?" he asked, a little sullenly, truth be told.

"I do not know," Rose answered. "This path has never led me to this place before."

That sounded even more worrisome, especially with the wisps of mist swirling around them, making it hard to see. "Then let's go someplace else, then," Tim suggested. "Somewhere you know."

"We must stay on the path, Timothy. Once we have begun to walk our road, we must walk it all the way or we are lost. And all may be lost."

The cold and clammy mist grew alarmingly thick, as if someone had turned on a fog machine full blast. "Rose?" Tim called. He could no longer see her. "Dr. Occult?"

"Still here." Rose's voice came out of the mist.

"I can't see the path!" Tim called. "Or you. Or Yo-yo!"

"I'm here," Rose replied, but her voice was muffled. Tim couldn't tell what direction it came from. Afraid that she would get too far ahead of him, he quickened his pace.

"Ooof!" Tim stumbled over a thick root and fell face forward into the dirt. He scrambled back up again, and discovered the mist had vanished.

And so had Rose.

Tim searched for his glasses, which had

fallen when he tripped. His fingers wrapped around them and he quickly put them back on. Luckily, they weren't broken, just a little bent. But even with his glasses on, Rose was still gone. He hadn't been *completely* abandoned, however: Yo-yo was perched on a nearby tree limb.

"Rose!" Tim called. "Dr. Occult!"

No answer.

Tim boosted himself up on the limb and sat beside Yo-yo. "Can you believe this?" he muttered. "She was the one who told *us* not to get lost. And now she's gone and lost herself. Himself. Oh, whatever! At least we've still got the path."

Now that the mist had evaporated, the path was clear again. Tim studied it, peering into the distance where it disappeared into a thick grove of trees. "What do you think?" he asked the owl. "Should we wait for him here? I mean, for *her*? Or should we go on?"

Yo-yo's yellow eyes didn't even blink.

"Fat lot of good you are. What the heck. It's cold just sitting here. He'll find us. Or *she'll* find us. Whichever."

Tim eased himself off the tree limb, carefully avoiding the jutting roots, and set out on the path again. "I don't know about you, Yo-yo," he said, "but I'm starving. I could eat a horse. An elephant, even."

"Tim!" a voice cried out. "Come here! Hurry!"

Tim's head whipped around in the direction of the man's voice. A few yards away, Dr. Occult stood outside a little cabin, his back to Tim, his trench coat a familiar and welcome sight.

"Dr. Occult!" Tim exclaimed. He headed toward the man. "You're a bloke again! How did you get ahead of me?"

"No time to explain. Quickly! It's an emergency!"

Tim raised a foot, about to step from the path, and froze. *Wasn't that one of Dr. Occult's rules? Don't leave the path no matter what?* Tim put his foot back down.

"Hurry, Tim! We're in great danger!" Dr. Occult called again.

Tim had not heard that kind of urgency in Dr. Occult's voice before. It must be serious. And wasn't the *first* rule that he had to obey any order Dr. Occult gave him? Wouldn't *that* rule supercede all the others? He had to risk it.

He leaped off the path and ran toward Dr. Occult, across the meadow. "What is it?" he panted as he came close to the man, who still had his back to him. "What's wrong?"

The man whirled around, and as he did, he transformed. A hag in tattered rags, with wild gray hair, scrawny arms, and pointy yellowed teeth, stood before Tim.

"What's wrong?" she cackled. "You've stepped off the path, boychick. That's what's wrong!"

With a swift move, she grabbed Tim's wrist. She clutched it so tightly he was afraid she'd snap it off. Giving him a sharp tug, he stumbled toward her. Up close, he could smell her foul breath, see the hairs poking up from the warts on her chin and nose. And all the while, he felt her fingernails, sharp as claws, digging into his skin.

"Dr. Occult?" Tim whispered. "Have you, uh, changed again?"

The woman laughed hysterically. "There is no Dr. Occult here, boychick! Just the Baba Yaga. And the Baba Yaga played a good trick on you!"

"Let me go!" Tim shouted, trying to tug his wrist from her grasp.

"Now what's Baba Yaga caught for herself, then? Is it a stew? Is it a roast? Is it blood pudding? Is it the tenderest of cutlets? Oh yes. All of them. Juicy and meaty and sweet."

Gross! Tim cringed. She was actually drooling! "You better let me go," he insisted, trying to sound brave and sure. "Dr. Occult is my protector. He'll find you. You'll be in big trouble."

"Find us? I doubt it." Baba Yaga swept Tim up into her powerful arms as if he were mere kindling for the fire. She easily carried him into her hut.

"Baba Yaga's little house is in the heart of the wild forest, and it will not be found in the same place two days running."

How can that be? Tim wondered. *How can her house change locations?* It wasn't as if she lived in a mobile home that could pack up and move to the next trailer park.

Baba Yaga stood in the center of her hut, still holding Tim. "Now, my house," she ordered, "do your wandering."

Gripped in Baba Yaga's strong arms, Tim felt the house lurch. Slowly, awkwardly, it rose into the air.

"What's doing that?" he cried.

Baba Yaga let out a shrieking laugh and carried Tim to the window. "My house has legs! Take a good look. You'll see none other like it in all of Faerie."

She grabbed Tim by the ankles and lowered him upside down out the window. His eyes nearly popped out of his head. The house was on top of a pair of chicken legs. He could see the huge clawed feet as they took great big steps forward.

She's not kidding, he realized with horror. *There's no way for Rose to find me.*

Baba Yaga dragged Tim back into the hut, banging his head on the windowsill as she did. No matter how much Tim squirmed or kicked or fought, her strong grip never loosened. It seemed that she didn't feel the slightest resistance.

"You're a thin one, but there's a little bit of meat on those ribs. Good!" she declared, slamming him onto a table and poking his side. She flipped him over and smacked his butt. "Steak on that rump. Good!" When she turned Tim over again, he realized she'd wrapped him in twine. She was tying him up!

"And heart to chew." Baba Yaga tossed him over her shoulder and carried him to the fireplace. She lifted him up and hung him, upside down, from a hook. "And eyes to suck and tongue to boil and eat piping hot." She tweaked his nose through the twine.

"I really think you ought to let me go," Tim said in as reasonable a tone as he could. He hoped being polite might win him some points. Seeing as he was trussed and hanging like a side of beef, he had no other options. Clearly he was no match for her in the strength department. Maybe the kids at home in London were right and he *was* a wimp.

"I'll be back soon, my juicy. Baba Yaga needs vegetables, yes. And herbs and kindling."

She grabbed a broomstick from the corner and crossed to the window. "Oooh, such feasting I will make. The grease will run down my chin, and I will crack your bones with my iron teeth to suck the marrow from within." It seemed she would faint with anticipation. She pulled herself together. "Window! Open you wide!"

The window did as it was commanded. Baba Yaga hopped aboard her broomstick and flew out.

"Oh, this isn't good," Tim moaned.

"I don't know," a small voice said nearby. "If she gets some nice crisp carrots, it might make for something quite passable."

Startled, Tim turned his head. He had thought he was alone in the hut. He found himself staring into the face of a rabbit that was hanging upside down beside him.

A talking rabbit!

Chapter Ten

"DID YOU—DID YOU say something?" Tim said to the rabbit. He felt foolish even asking the question, but so many strange things had happened so far, why not talking animals? He had definitely heard someone speak, and the rabbit was the only one it could be. Well, the rabbit or the little hedgehog hanging upside down next to the rabbit.

"Tsk tsk tsk," the rabbit tsk'd between its large front teeth. "You've done it this time, matey."

"What?" Tim asked.

"He's right, you know," the hedgehog said in a little squeak of a voice. "You're going to be stew."

"I mean, me and Master Redlaw here." The rabbit tipped its head toward the hedgehog. "We're fairly used to the idea of endin' up in a pot."

"So to speak, Master Leveret," the hedgehog

said, nodding its prickly head rapidly. "Although mostly us hedge-pigs is encased in clay and roasted in embers." He stretched his neck in an attempt to bring his face closer to Tim's. "On account of us havin' us prickles," he added in a confidential whisper.

"Stands corrected, Master Redlaw," the rabbit conceded. "Stands corrected and grateful to yer, I must say."

"Um . . ." Tim began, but then didn't know what else to say so he left it at that.

"Oooooh, blimey," the rabbit said. "We's forgettin' our manners again, matey. Must be something to do with hanging upside down. All that blood to the tips of the ears."

"Yes, yes, of course." The hedgehog nodded enthusiastically. Tim twisted to avoid being pricked by the hedgehog's spines.

"I'm Master Leveret," the rabbit said. "And this is Master Redlaw."

The hedgehog nodded. "That's me!"

"We is all she'd caught before she got you."

"And you might be?" asked Master Redlaw, the hedgehog.

"I'm Tim. Timothy Hunter."

First a gasp, then both animals chuckled. They looked at each other, and Tim had the distinct feeling that if they were untied—and human—they'd be slapping each other's backs over the joke they shared.

"A hunter, eh?" chortled Master Leveret the rabbit. "Well, then, this must be a might turn-around for you."

"Hah! Here's a hunter, and he's the one what's been hunted!" Master Redlaw guffawed. "And caught, I must say!"

"I'm not a hunter," Tim protested. "It's just my name."

"Oh, lad, we know all about names. Just so long as you don't hunt hares, I won't make issue of it, laddie."

"Or hedge-pigs," Master Redlaw added. "I won't be standing for people who'd be hunting hedge-pigs. Because of me taking it personally, don'tcha know."

"Well, sure," Tim said. "I'm taking this pretty personally myself."

A sudden flutter and a dark shape by the window caught their attention. Yo-yo flew into the hut.

"Yo-yo!" Tim cried.

"It's an owl, Master Redlaw," said Master Leveret.

"Remarkable," the hedgehog exclaimed. "That was my thought exactly, Master Leveret. Blow me down, I thought. If that doesn't seem to be an owl."

"When was the last time you spent any time with an owl?" Master Leveret asked.

"Come to think of it, never. But perhaps—"

"Be quiet, you two," Tim begged the chattering animals. He turned to address the owl. "Yo-yo, can you get a message to Dr. Occult? I mean, Rose? Tell her—or him—whatever he is now—where I am and to come and get us!"

"Whooo!" Yo-yo replied.

Yo-yo didn't move. He and Tim stared at each other. Tim was the first one to blink. "Well, Yo-yo, go on."

"What your owl said, if you'll pardon me translaterin' for you," offered Master Leveret, "is that it's terrible afraid it wouldn't know where to find the lady or gentleman in question."

"That's what it was a-sayin' right enough," the hedgehog agreed, nodding vigorously.

"You got all that from 'whoo'?" Tim asked.

All three creatures stared at Tim as if he were a complete dolt.

Tim flushed. It was bad enough to be shown up in gym class. Being treated like an idiot by a rabbit, a hedgehog, and an owl, well, that was a new and highly unpleasant experience for him.

"Okay, that's what Yo-yo said," Tim agreed. "Yo-yo, listen, that old woman—"

"She's not an old woman," Master Leveret interrupted, a long ear twitching.

"She's the Baba Yaga," Master Redlaw added, as if that meant anything comprehensible.

"Ooooh, she'd spit if she heard you call her an old woman."

"Fine. That—*Baba Yaga*—wants to eat me." He heard a sniff and a throat being cleared beside him and quickly added, "Eat *all* of us, that is. She just went off to get some herbs."

"Probably chives," said the rabbit. "And thyme. And bay leaves, I expects. And cow butter, for the sauces."

"We hedge-pigs don't hold with that fancy stuff," Master Redlaw said disdainfully. "My granny used to say, no one ever used fancy foreign sauces on a hedge-pig. Clay and embers is what you gets, and a little salt, if yer lucky."

"Can you please be quiet!" Tim snapped. "Sheesh! You'd think you were looking forward to being the main ingredient in a recipe."

"If she has a good hand with the thyme, I wouldn't mind so," the rabbit said.

"Don't want any of those fancy foreign heavy sauces," the hedgehog grumbled. "Not if she knows a thing or two about good eating."

"Yo-yo," Tim tried again, "can't you cut the ropes with your beak or something?"

Yo-yo flew in a circle around Tim. "Whoo," he said.

Tim looked to Master Leveret for translation. "It says it doesn't think so," the rabbit said.

So this is it, Tim thought. *I've made a complete mess of things, and now I'm going to be cooked into a stew. Trussed like an animal and heavily seasoned. What a way to go.*

"Yo-yo," Tim said bravely. "If you see Dr. Occult again, tell him I'm sorry I stepped off the path. And that I wish I'd never started on this magic stuff. And tell him to say good-bye to my dad for me. And Molly. She can have my entire comic book collection. She should like that. Okay?"

"Whoo."

"It said, fair enough," said Master Leveret. He sounded sad, and Tim wasn't sure if the rabbit was feeling sorry for him or if Master Leveret was translating the owl's feelings along with his words.

"You know," Master Redlaw ventured. "There is a remarkable peculiar thing about yon hooty-owl."

"You mean it bein' out in the daytime when everybody knows owls is nighttime folks?" asked Master Leveret.

"Why, that's exceedin' perspicious of you. But no. What I was thinking was more in the nature of the chain wrapped around itself that is out of the ordinary."

"It's just a chain we got at the market," Tim explained. "Nothing special. Yo-yo picked it out from a pile of junk." What did any of this matter anyway? he wondered. Were they just keeping themselves entertained until the Baba Yaga came back to cook them? If so, maybe they could come up with something a little more distracting.

"'Just a chain'?" said Master Redlaw. "That's Empusa's Infinitely Extensible, that is! Now there's a thing. Empusa's Infinitely Extensible Chain a-wrapped around an owl!"

"What are you talking about?" Tim asked.

"Famous it is, matey!" the hedgehog exhorted. "One of Empusa's lost treasures, right up there with the Drum Unescapable, and the Heliotrope Gamahaean Union."

"Well, paint me pink and call me a noodle," exclaimed the rabbit. "If I didn't completely miss the point of what you was getting at earlier. You must think me a right old puddin' head."

"Think nothing of it, Master Leveret," said Master Redlaw graciously. "Us hedge-piggies are natural born thinkers."

"So is this going to rescue us?" Tim asked. Hope was returning, even if the circulation in his arms wasn't.

"No, laddie, no. I can't with all honesty say that it will," admitted the hedgehog.

"But it's a definite something to tell yer grandchildren, eh, Master Redlaw?" The rabbit ahemed and then affected a very pompous tone: "'Coincidentally, the very same day I was popped into a cookpot I discovered Empusa's Infinitely Extensible Chain on an owl.'" The rabbit laughed. "Now that'd be some story."

"Although, that being said," Master Redlaw offered, "if that there owl was to fly down to the underside of the Baba Yaga's little hut, and if it was to wrap the chain around the legs of the house . . ."

"And wrap 'em and wrap 'em and wrap 'em, it being infinitely extensible, like . . ." said Master Leveret, his ears waggling in excitement.

"Until—thump—over it'd topple," cheered the hedgehog.

Tim's eyes widened as he understood what the animals were suggesting. It might actually work!

"And then we'd just need to figure out how to undo all these knots. And then us'd all climb through a window and we'd be off into the long grass and gone before you could say Januarius Gammadion Fontarabia Dagonet Knipperdollings," continued the hedgehog.

"Just the ticket!" said the rabbit.

"Brilliant!" Tim exclaimed. He faced the owl. "What do you think, Yo-yo? Can you do it?"

Yo-yo gave a little hoot, and hurried out the window in a flurry of brown-tipped feathers.

Tim wished he could see what was happening. Were the little animals right? Was that junky chain really some incredible special extensible thinga-ma-whazits—and their way out of this mess?

The rabbit and the hedgehog must have been thinking along the same lines. They had actually stopped talking, waiting to see what would happen. Their big round eyes just stared at the window.

Then the whole house came to a sudden, bone-shattering stop. *If we were in a car*, Tim thought, *we'd all have whiplash!* With a sickening, lurching motion, the house tumbled sideways to the ground, making an enormous crash that Tim imagined could be heard through all of Faerie.

Tim landed hard, slamming into the floor, all the air knocked out of him. But then he realized three important things: (1) He wasn't dead, (2) his glasses were still in one piece, and best of all, (3) the crash loosened his ropes enough to free his hands!

Yo-yo swooped back into the hut, hooting with

obvious pride. Tim twisted his face up from the floor.

"You did it!" he cheered Yo-yo. "You stopped the house! And look!" He wiggled his fingers at Yo-yo. "Help me get out of these ropes."

Yo-yo tugged and Tim squirmed, and finally the bindings broke apart. Tim leaped up and scouted around the little hut. Everything—furniture, tools, odds and ends—had all slid down to one side. It was quite a mess. He spotted what he was looking for. "Perfect!" He grabbed a sharp knife and cut down the rabbit and hedgehog. "There you go," he said.

"Thanks ever so," said Master Redlaw the hedgehog.

"Yes, much obliged," added Master Leveret the rabbit.

Yo-yo hooted from the windowsill.

"Beggin' yer pardon," said the rabbit, "but the owl says we ought to get out of here something rapid. She's coming back."

"Then let's go!" Tim carefully climbed out of the toppled hut. Master Leveret and Master Redlaw crept out behind him and jumped down to the grass.

"My house!" Baba Yaga shrieked above them. "What have you done to my poor house?" She circled overhead on her broomstick.

Tim picked up Master Redlaw and ran. Master Leveret bounded beside them, and Yo-yo flew.

"I'll eat them alive!" Baba Yaga screamed.

"Come on, laddie," the hedgehog encouraged from under Tim's arm. "Keep it up! Keep running."

Tim tripped over a gnarled root. He sprawled face forward on the ground. *What is it about this place?* he thought. *I'm not this clumsy at home! Are the trees out to get me?* He tried to stand but discovered his ankle was tangled in some vines.

Master Redlaw had gone flying when Tim fell. "Need some help, lad?" the hedgehog asked, crawling back toward Tim.

"No!" Tim shouted. "Run! Get out of here!"

"Are you—" Master Leveret began.

"Just go!"

"On your insisterance," said the hedgehog.

"Wouldn't want to upset the lad," added the rabbit.

Master Leveret dashed into the bushes. Master Redlaw crept into the tall grass. Tim was glad that at least the little critters had escaped.

Tim tried to crawl, shaking his leg, desperate to untangle his ankle from the snarl of vines.

"Whoopsie!" Baba Yaga cackled. Tim could hear that she was much closer. Just a few feet away. "Now up we gets, laddie. Come on."

Slowly, Tim turned to face the hag.

And discovered Rose standing between him and Baba Yaga.

"Out of my way, woman!" Baba Yaga shouted. "That brat is my dinner. And he's hurt my little house."

"Timothy is under my protection in this realm," Rose answered calmly. "I charge you to trouble him no more."

"He's mine! And you dare order me? Why I should—"

Rose cut her off. "I know your true name," she declared. "Do you want me to shout it now so that all the animals of the forest, all the birds of the air, every passing nixie and goblin will know it too? Your name will be as common as crabgrass. Would you like that, Baba Yaga?"

"You're lying!" Baba Yaga shrieked. "You do not know my name."

"Perhaps. Do you wish to find out how loudly I can shout?"

Baba Yaga seemed to shrink a little. "No," she grumbled, her voice low. Her broomstick dropped a few inches.

"Then do you discharge all obligation and lien on the boy?"

"I do." Baba Yaga was positively sulking.

"Good."

Tim watched the old hag fly away. Once she was completely out of sight, he unsnarled his ankle and stood up. "You were bluffing, weren't you?" Tim asked Rose.

"What?" She looked puzzled.

"Like John Constantine in that nightclub. You were just bluffing. About knowing her name."

"No, Tim. I wasn't bluffing."

Tim got the distinct impression that not only wasn't Rose bluffing, she strongly disapproved of it as a tactic.

"When I was younger I learned certain matters," Rose explained. "Among them were names. Names of gods, and mortals, and wild folks. Names of cities, and trees. Of eagles and serpents. I was not bluffing. I would have destroyed her."

"Oh." Tim felt funny inside. He felt honored that she would have used that power and knowledge to save him. But he hated that he had put her in a position where she'd have to. He didn't want to be some blundering kid who always needed bailing out.

They found the path again and walked along it in silence, as Yo-yo flew above them. The woods were full of sounds, but no words passed between Rose and Tim for some time. Each was deep in thought. Tim couldn't even begin to guess what was in Rose's mind. Probably wishing they'd chosen some other kid to show magic to.

Then came an unmistakable sound: thundering hoofs. Coming toward them swiftly. A beautiful woman rode around the bend a few yards in front of them. A beautiful *green* woman. She reined in her enormous white horse and came to a stop.

"Who be ye? And what do ye on this path? Speak! Lest I change ye to scuttling mice and set your own owl upon ye!"

Chapter Eleven

TIM SIGHED. COULDN'T he make a move without being threatened? Was everyone in Faerie out to get him? This place seemed even more dangerous than his own world, where all those magic practitioners wanted to kill him. That, at least, would be a simple fate. Here, who knew what could happen to him? Snout wanted to make him a servant for seventy years; the "heart's desire" seller wanted his fingers, or his eye color; Baba Yaga wanted to cook him. There were probably as many possible fates in this world as there were creatures who could think them up. Tim's hands balled up into fists and his whole body tensed. Not from fear, though. Not this time.

Rose laid a hand on his arm. She must have sensed his frustration. "My lady," she addressed the green woman. "We are travelers. And we needs must walk this path wherever it will lead us."

Needs must? Tim squinted at Rose. She'd gone all medieval. He shrugged. That must be how they liked to speak here in Faerie. All fancy.

"Who rides the wind must go where their steed will take them," the woman on the horse responded.

"Who treads the way of stars must walk in silence," Rose replied.

Now Tim out and out stared. What the heck was going on? Were they speaking in code?

"I see," the woman on the horse said. "We have met before, have we not?"

"Yes, lady," answered Rose.

So they *were* speaking in code, Tim thought. It was like some magical password.

"The last time we met you wore a man's skin," the lady on horseback said. "And you looked out at the world through male eyes."

"Yes, lady."

"Ah."

They must have passed the test, Tim thought, and this lady seemed to approve of both versions of Rose, because she smiled. "Will you introduce me to your companion?" she asked.

"As you wish, lady. This lad is called Timothy Hunter. Timothy, this lady is Queen of this realm."

Tim gaped at the green lady. Then, remembering his etiquette, he dropped to one knee before the horse. "Pleased to meet you, um, your Majesty." That's how one was supposed to address royals, wasn't it? He never imagined that he'd meet a queen by *leaving* Britain! Much less a beautiful *green* queen!

"You may call me Titania," the lady said. She studied him for a moment. "I can see that you have undergone trials in my land, child."

Does it show? Tim wondered. He raked his fingers through his dark hair, trying to make it lie flat. He hoped he wasn't a filthy mess; after hanging upside down in Baba Yaga's hut and then landing facedown in the dirt, it was a definite possibility.

"Let me assure you," Titania said, "it is not all hardship here. There are delights aplenty in this place."

"Yes, your Majesty." Tim nodded.

The lady smiled at him, and Tim felt shot through with warmth. Her eyes seemed to change color, and her green skin sparkled as if she wore glitter. He thought he had never seen a more beautiful woman in his life.

"You came here seeking me," Titania said. Tim noticed her voice had a lilt to it, somewhere between singing and speaking.

"Did we?" Tim asked. "I thought we were just following the path."

"This is my realm, and all paths in it are my paths."

The horse snorted impatiently, and the woman patted it and murmured a few sharp words that Tim couldn't understand. The horse settled back down.

"What will you have him know, Rose Spiritus?" the Queen asked Rose.

"It has been given to me to show Tim the spheres beyond mortal ken," Rose replied.

"And you have shown him Faerie?" The Queen seemed flattered. "Good. We will go to my palace."

"Is it far?" Tim asked. He didn't want to sound rude, but he was tired of all this walking. His feet were sore, and he was bruised from tumbling over in Baba Yaga's hut. Being tied up and hung upside down waiting to be cooked really took it out of a bloke. He could use a nap.

"It is as close as the harvest moon in the evening sky," the Queen said. "As distant as a dream on wakening. Near as a rainbow, and so remote you could walk forever and never reach it. Is it far? No, Timothy, it is not far."

They were there. They were simply, astonishingly, there. Tim glanced up at Titania on her horse, surprised. How had she done it? How had it happened? To him, it seemed as if they had never moved at all.

"Welcome to my home," Titania said, gesturing to the shimmering castle in front of them.

Tim looked up at the high turrets, which glittered like icicles in sunlight. There was something familiar about everything he had seen in Faerie. Then he realized why. The architecture, the clothing, even some of the language—it all reminded him of the past. The past where Merlin the great magician had lived. The past he had studied in school. The time when there were kings and queens and courts and courtiers and damsels in distress. Only, the inhabitants here were an amazing mix ranging from the almost human to the completely unrecognizable.

A yellow groomsman with an upturned nose and tufts of purple hair on the tops of his purple ears appeared. He held out his hand and helped Titania dismount. Then he took the horse's reins and led it away.

"Shall I show you my grounds?" Titania asked, smiling. Now that she was standing beside him, Tim could see that she was tall and willowy—taller even than Rose. Her flowing burgundy gown skimmed the grass and gracefully floated around her slim frame with her movements. Her long, green hair hung down to the middle of her back, and with every step she took, little bells jangled from the ribbons twined through her shining strands.

"Please," Tim said. "That sounds like fun."

Rose and Tim walked with Titania across the tiled portico in front of the castle. A low wall separated the front court from the main entryway, which had a mosaic walk leading to the castle door. A brilliant blue pool on either side reflected the cloudless sky. Yo-yo darted about, first flying ahead, then over to the pools by the castle, then circling above them.

Rounding the castle, they passed formal gardens, surrounded by ornate gates, and then the grounds opened up into lush meadows. Up ahead, Tim saw a group on horseback, and what seemed to be a picnic under enormous leafy trees.

"Ah," Titania said. "My husband has not yet left. You should meet him."

Tim gulped. Titania's husband? If she was a queen, that meant her husband was . . . He was about to meet a king! He hoped he wouldn't say anything wrong. Or dumb.

Titania, Rose, and Tim reached the picnickers by the trees. It was a group of creatures Titania called sprites and flitlings. From what Tim could tell, flitlings were the tiny beings that he thought of as fairy-book fairies—they were pretty little things with wings. The sprites looked almost like regular people, if people were always pretty and handsome and came in all the colors of the rainbow.

One of the sprites had a lute and was entertaining the others. He stopped singing as Titania approached, and several of the flitlings giggled. They looked just the way Tim and Molly did when they were about to be caught drawing terrible caricatures of their teachers. Tim's eyes flicked to Titania. He had the feeling the sprite had been making up rude songs about her.

Titania acted as if she hadn't noticed a thing. "Beautiful day," she greeted the group.

"Yes, Majesty," the singer said. Several of the group quickly stood and bowed.

Titania waved a hand. "No need," she said. "Be as you were. I am here just a moment."

Titania stepped away from the group and watched the figures on horseback. She seemed to be waiting for them to notice her.

Tim watched, fascinated, as the elegant and stately queen began acting like a teenage girl being ignored at a dance. She fiddled with her hair. She rolled her eyes and tapped her foot. She rearranged the folds of her dress several times. She crossed her arms over her chest and pouted.

Finally, a man on a large white horse trotted over. Tim couldn't help staring. Not only was the man blue, but he had what looked like curved ram's horns on his head.

"Well met, Titania," the man greeted her, pulling his horse to a stop.

"Husband," she replied, sounding bored and unconcerned.

Tim smiled. *What an act.*

The blue man noticed Rose and Tim. "I see you have guests."

"Ah, yes. Rose Spiritus, Timothy Hunter, this is my husband, King Auberon."

"Your Majesty," Rose said, bowing her head.

Tim took the cue from Rose; falling to bended knee wasn't required. "Pleased to meet you, sire," Tim said, dipping his chin to his chest.

"Will you join us for some further conversation by the back pool?" Titania asked.

"I am off to the hunt," Auberon said.

"Again?" Titania said.

Auberon's jaw tightened. "I find pleasure with my friends," he said. "They treat me with warmth and respect."

"And I do not?" Titania demanded.

Uh-oh. It sounded like a domestic squabble to Tim. He noticed that the sprites and flitlings kept their distance.

"You were invited," Auberon said.

"Because you knew I would not join you," Titania countered.

"If it amuses you to entertain these guests, go right ahead. I have other plans." With that, Auberon turned his horse and rejoined his friends. They trotted away, toward the woods, hounds barking at their heels.

Titania's eyes narrowed as she watched them. Then she spun around. "We will return to the castle. Now."

Fighting with her husband sure makes her pick up speed, Tim observed, struggling to keep up with the vexed Queen of Faerie. Rose's legs were longer than Tim's, so she was better able to keep up the pace. By the time they reached the large tiled patio behind the castle, Tim was breathing hard.

"Please, make yourself comfortable," Titania instructed. Tim lowered himself to a nearby sofa awkwardly, wishing he had something to say. Looking up, he spotted a bird flying far overhead.

"Look!" he said, pointing to the bird. "That's my owl, Yo-yo. I'd wondered where he'd gone to!"

"That is no bird of yours," Titania corrected him sharply.

Tim, Rose, and Titania watched the bird as it swooped toward them. Titania was right; that bird wasn't Yo-yo. It was much larger, much more powerful.

"A handsome falcon," Rose commented.

"Yes," Titania replied, a smile slowly spreading across her face. "Yes, he is that."

The falcon was now circling just above them. Titania's expression changed. She looked up at the bird. "Not now," she snapped.

Instantly, the falcon flew off. *If she used that tone on me*, Tim thought, *I would be off as well*. He snuck a peek at Titania. *She may be beautiful, but she sure is moody*.

The Queen had settled onto a couch, arranging her dress prettily around her. She ran her fingers through her hair, setting the little bells chiming. She smiled at Tim; a full and radiant smile.

"You have been seeing worlds, child," Titania said. "You know, there are many realms accessible from your world, as well as mine."

"Really?" Tim asked. "How many?"

"An infinite number. Waiting to be opened." She held out her hand. A thick old-fashioned-looking key glittered between her fingers. "Here is the key. Use it how you will. A gift from me to you."

She threw the key at Tim, who caught it easily.

"No!" Rose gasped.

Chapter Twelve

"Did I do something wrong?" Tim asked Rose. The key felt warm and heavy in his hand. It felt right—as if it belonged there. So why was Rose so upset? "Did I do something wrong?" he repeated.

Rose had shut her eyes and held her hands to her face.

"No," Titania answered for Rose. "No, you did nothing wrong."

She is so beautiful, Tim thought, looking at the Queen. *How can someone green be so pretty?*

Titania crossed to a small table and rang a little bell. Instantly, a servant stepped into the room.

"Hamnett, two strawberry cordials," Titania ordered. "One for me and one for my guest, Timothy."

"Oh, none for me," Tim said hastily.

Titania smiled. "Ah, so you do know the rules

of Faerie. Well then, just one. For me."

The servant slipped away, and Titania kept her large, ever-changing eyes on Tim. "You are interested in other realms?" she asked.

Tim shrugged. "Sure, they're pretty cool." He liked how nonchalant he sounded. Kind of like John Constantine.

"You can access an infinite number from Faerie," Titania told him.

"Really?" Tim asked. "Do you go through a little fence in the middle of a field?"

"No, child. You go through a door. By using a key." Titania nodded at the key Tim held in his hand. "Come."

She stood and led Tim and Rose behind the castle, to a row of gigantic doors that seemed to stretch to the horizon. Between the doors were more of the low sofas that were scattered around the patio. Titania settled herself on one of them. Rose remained standing.

"Those all lead to worlds?" Tim asked, his voice dropped to a whisper.

"Yes, for one who can open them."

Tim whirled around to look at Rose. She gave a small nod, and he stepped forward, drawn to a glowing golden door. He inserted the key into the lock. The door swung open.

Tim stood on the threshold of the new world.

He stared into a dark place, primeval, hot and humid. He detected bird caws and growls of creatures he could not identify. He heard Rose's voice behind him.

"This is Skartaris," she informed him. "In this world, time deforms and twists upon itself. Dinosaurs roam the earth, while planes fly overhead."

Weird. Tim stepped back and shut the door. He approached the next one. "Does this key fit all of them?" he asked.

"If you have the power to open them," Titania answered.

Do I? Tim wondered. He slid the key into the next lock. It turned. He suddenly knew—though he didn't know how he knew it—that he would be able to open the entire row of doors. And the doors to additional worlds inside them. He had that kind of power. He withdrew the key again and stared at it.

"It is time for us to leave," Rose said, laying a hand on Tim's shoulder.

Tim's head whipped around and he stared at her. "So soon?" He wanted to explore more worlds, check out what the palace was like, how the Queen of Faerie lived, what else there was to see in Faerie.

Titania looked pleased. She stretched out on

the low velvet couch. Now she reminded Tim of a cat, pausing before pouncing. And hadn't she threatened to turn him into a mouse when they met? He felt strangely nervous.

"Tim has far to go before his journey's end," said Rose. "We thank you for your hospitality, but we must return to our own world."

"Really?" Titania sat back up on the sofa. "Tim was told the rules of Faerie, wasn't he?"

Tim's gaze went back and forth between the two women; one a queen of an alternate world of fairy creatures, the other a woman who was also a man. They both seemed very powerful, strong. And on opposite sides of an argument he didn't quite understand.

Titania pointed at Tim. "There. In his hand. A gift from Faerie. He took it, did he not?"

She stood and strolled toward Tim, definitely in high cat mode. "Timothy, boy," she crooned, her hand gently stroking his face. "Will you stay with me? You will be my page and servant, here in the lands of summer's twilight, where there is no age or death." She lifted his chin so he could gaze directly into her eyes. They seemed to change color as he looked at them. Her touch was like a butterfly's, there and not there. Her voice was like the incense in Madame Xanadu's dark apartment, swirling around him, insinuating itself into him. Was that just a day ago? Or was it more? It would be nice to stay in one place for a while, he thought.

"You have not seen a fraction of the marvels of this world, Tim. You have not tasted our fruit, nor drunk our wine, nor danced to your soul's delight in our revelries."

Was she wearing perfume? Tim hadn't noticed before, but now he got the distinct impression of an intoxicating scent coming from her—flowers and spring breezes.

Her fingers left his chin and trailed down his arm. She held his hand lightly. "Stay. Be my page. I can teach you much."

What happened to all the birds? Tim wondered. Just a few minutes ago the air was filled with the sounds of birds, and insects chirping, and sprites giggling, and all manner of fairies singing. Now he felt he stood in a vacuum of silence. What had she asked him? Oh, yes. She wanted him to stay here and be her "page." *That's another word for a servant, isn't it?*

Tim coughed. Her perfume now seemed a little too strong. Maybe he was allergic; all he knew was, it was overly sweet, cloying.

"Thank you for your kind offer, your Majesty," he said as politely as he could. "But I want to go home. I don't want to stay here forever." Molly would never forgive him if he vanished without saying good-bye. *She'd miss me*, he thought. *And I would miss her.*

Queen Titania dropped his hand. He was relieved to see she didn't look angry or even disappointed. She took a step back.

"I am not offering a choice, Timothy," she said simply. "You took a gift from me. A silver key. A key that opens worlds."

Tim glanced down at the key in his hand, the truth coming at him hard. *She tricked me. I didn't accept it, she just threw it at me.* He dropped the key to the ground.

Titania's expression never changed. "You in your turn now owe a gift to me. Of equal value and worth. Otherwise I will be forced to keep you here."

"I want to go home," Tim insisted. "My dad needs me. And Molly. I mean, I'm nothing special. I want to go home."

"It's too late," Titania said. "Stay here because you choose it, or stay here against your will. Or give me a gift as precious as the key that opens worlds."

"Why would you give me something so valuable?" Tim demanded.

Titania didn't answer, just waited for his response.

"I apologize for this, Timothy," Rose said. She

stepped up behind Tim and placed her hands on his shoulders. "I wish you had heeded my warning. But do not despair."

Tim sighed with relief. Of course, Rose would get him out of this.

"I will return with the other three," she promised. "We will free you somehow, even if we have to raze half of Faerie to do so."

Tim glanced at Titania. She didn't seem to register the threat. He craned his neck and looked up at Rose, as he understood what this meant. "You mean, you aren't going to stop her?"

"I cannot," Rose said. "But you are our responsibility and we will do what we can."

"But—"

"Rules are rules, here as much as anywhere else," Rose said. "You have her gift in your possession."

Tim bent down and snatched the key from the ground. He held it out to Titania. "Here. I don't want it anyway."

Titania shook her head, the bells in her hair jangling. "Once given, a gift cannot be taken back."

"I'm not staying here!" Tim shouted. "This is ridiculous. I'm human! I don't belong here!"

"Then what will you give me in exchange?" Titania asked. "You see, I'm reasonable. If you have something to trade, I will accept it."

Tim racked his brain but knew he'd come up empty. "I don't have anything special. Even the thing I got at the market was just normal. That Glory bloke said so."

"What did you get at the market?" Titania asked.

"An ordinary egg," Tim replied, fishing it out of his pocket. He was surprised that it hadn't broken in all of his adventures. It was sturdier than it looked. "That's what he called it."

The egg glowed in his hand. Sparks swirled inside like the tiny constellations he had seen with the Stranger.

"A Mundane Egg!" Titania gasped.

Tim glanced up. "That's what I meant. Normal. Boring. Mundane. I got good grades on my synonyms. I knew it was one of those words."

"No, Timothy," Rose corrected softly. "It isn't one of those words at all. Not in this context."

"Why?" Tim asked. "What's so special about it?"

"Inside this egg is a part of creation as yet unborn," Rose explained. "One day the egg will hatch, and from it a whole world will emerge. Every world is hatched from a Mundane Egg. And they are valuable. Almost beyond measure."

Tim stared down at the egg in his hand. He

held something that contained entire universes?

"Your Majesty," Rose addressed Titania. "I ask that you do us the honor of accepting Timothy's gift."

Tim held out the egg to Titania. "Please?"

"I have no choice. Rules are rules." The Queen carefully lifted the egg from Tim's hand. "Strange. I had thought the last Mundane Egg hatched long since."

"So you'll take it?" Tim asked.

"Very well," Titania said, her eyes never leaving the egg. "You may go—both of you."

Rose took Tim's arm and they left the palace. Outside, they found the path and continued on, Yo-yo circling above them again.

Titania watched them as they disappeared into the grove. The falcon reappeared overhead. It swooped down to land on the railing near Titania. In seconds the powerful bird transformed into a man. His long straight hair was a little lighter than Tim's, his face sculpted and lean.

Titania turned to him. "You were right about the boy, Tamlin," Titania said thoughtfully. "He is special. He is to be watched."

Tim woke up in a field, grass tickling his face.

"Wha—What?" He sat up and looked around. He lay beside the gate through which they entered

Faerie. Rose was standing over him, transformed back into Dr. Occult, trench coat, hat, and all.

"We're back," Tim said.

"That's right."

Tim gave Dr. Occult a suspicious look. "We're not somewhere funny, are we? Alternative universe or something?"

Dr. Occult looked tired. "No, it's over. This part of the journey, anyway."

Tim glanced down at his hand. He was still holding the key. "What do I do with this?" he asked.

"It's yours," Dr. Occult said. "It was a fair trade, after all. Keep it. Perhaps you'll find a door that key will fit."

Tim stood and stretched. Yo-yo sat perched on the gate post, watching him. "Shall we?" Tim said to the bird. Yo-yo flew to his shoulder. They crossed the stream and Tim found the spot where he'd buried his coins and his house keys. After retrieving them, they headed toward the horizon, where the sun was rising.

"Well, that's over," Tim said with a yawn.

"This part of your travels, yes."

"Only one more journey to go, then," Tim said. "Only one more guide. The blind guy— Mister E."

"That's right."

"So where now?" Tim asked.

"Tomorrow."

"That's when we leave?"

"No, Timothy," Dr. Occult replied. "That's not *when* you're going. It's *where* you're going."

Chapter Thirteen

JOHN CONSTANTINE leaned against the wall and glared at the rain. He and Mister E had taken cover in a dark doorway. The Stranger seemed oblivious to the weather and continued his slow pace up and down the sidewalk.

"I heard a joke about you once, E," Constantine said.

"A joke?"

"I think it was a joke. Bloke I met in a bar in Katmandu said you always carried a pocket full of stakes in case you met a vampire, and a gun loaded with silver bullets, in case you ever met a werewolf."

Without a word, Mister E pulled a pointed wooden stake from inside his trench coat.

Involuntarily, Constantine took a step back. "Blimey," he exclaimed. "I take it you hammer first and ask questions afterward."

"The only good vampire is a dead vampire, Constantine."

"Hate to argue a point, but aren't they all dead by definition?"

"Fool." Mister E slipped the stake back into his coat.

"You ought to watch it, you know," Constantine warned. "One day the bogeymen are going to come out of their closets and start parading down the high street. They'll be marching for equal rights, and your head on a platter as their worst oppressor."

"Is that meant to be funny?" Mister E snarled.

"If you're lucky." John held out a pack of cigarettes toward the blind man. "Smoke?"

"Unlike you, I do not defile the temple of my body."

"Probably sworn off caffeine too," Constantine muttered. "And sweets."

"Quiet," the Stranger said. "They are returning."

Tim spotted Constantine right away, his blond head unprotected from the rain. The two others seemed to blend more into the shadows.

"Hullo, Tim!" John greeted him. "How was Fairyland?"

"I'm not sure I remember it properly," Tim admitted. "It's all gone a bit fuzzy, like a dream. I sort of remember it, but I don't think I can talk about it. Not in any way that would make sense."

"Are you hungry?" asked the Stranger. "Do you need rest? Or are you ready for your final journey?"

"I don't know. I guess so. I guess I'm ready." Tim hadn't felt ready for any of his previous adventures, and so now he asked himself why he should feel any more ready for this one. He jerked his head toward Mister E, who was looming silently in the doorway. "I suppose he's going to be my guide."

"Yes." Mister E nodded. "I am also ready."

"Okay, Yo-yo," Tim said to his owl. "Ready to go to tomorrow?"

"No," Mister E ordered. "The owl is a bird of darkness and night. It will stay here."

This guy is seriously uptight, Tim thought. But he realized that there were probably more rules where they were going, and Mister E would know them better than he did.

"Tim?" Dr. Occult said.

Tim sighed. He would have liked having Yo-yo along for company. "Okay. You stay here, then," he told the owl. He looked at Dr. Occult. "You'll take care of him, right?"

Dr. Occult nodded.

Everyone seemed a lot more serious this time. It made Tim nervous. *Maybe it's just because this is their last chance to show me stuff*, Tim told

himself, *and if I don't learn it all now, I never will.*
He guessed that the pressure was on them too.

"Take my arm," said Mister E.

"I thought if you were . . . well, blind," Tim
said, "then you'd want to hold onto *my* arm."

"Where we're going, it is you who will be
walking blind. I know the path. Now close your
eyes."

Tim squeezed his eyes shut.

"Step forward, child," Mister E instructed.

"Just walk?"

"Yes, and keep your eyes tightly closed as you
walk, until I tell you to halt and to open them."

"Where are we going? Are you going to show
me my future?"

"Possibly, boy. Keep walking."

Tim placed one foot in front of the other, very
aware of the looming presence of Mister E beside
him. He didn't feel anything. Not the stomach-
wrenching whoosh that he'd felt when he was
taken to the past with the Stranger. Not the disorienting instantaneous travel he'd experienced
with John Constantine, nor the strangeness he felt
when walking through the gate with Dr. Occult.
He was now just blindly placing one foot in front
of the other.

Blind. Tim wondered if this was the way Mister
E felt all the time. He had no way of knowing what

was in front of him, behind him, around him. He was vulnerable. Tim shivered. He didn't like the feeling.

"We are fifteen years into your future," Mister E said. "Or one of them. You may open your eyes."

Just like that? Tim's eyes flicked open. "What do you mean, 'or one of them'?" he asked Mister E.

"There are very few stable futures, boy."

Tim looked around—and instantly wanted to shut his eyes again. They were at the scene of some sort of crime—or massacre. There were bodies, and blood, and screams all around them. Funny, he hadn't heard anything until he'd opened his eyes. Maybe if he shut them again, the wails and moans and shouts would stop. No. Tim shuddered, closing his eyes and then reopening them. *That doesn't help. Not at all.*

"The future is a series of infinitely branching possibilities," Mister E said, as if completely unconcerned by the destruction and mayhem around him. He dragged Tim forward, deeper into the scene. "When we walk it, we walk down the most probable paths, those with the greatest likelihood of occurring."

"So . . . so it's likely I'll wind up in this terrible place?" Tim asked, his eyes scanning the scene. A deserted warehouse, dark streets, garbage, bodies. More bodies. More blood.

"But we aren't really traveling to the future, are we?" Tim asked. "This is like when I went to the past, right? We're just observing. Nothing can happen to us here. They can't see us."

"No," Mister E said. "We are truly in the future. One of them."

They had come around a corner. Tim ducked as a lightning bolt shot toward his head. He threw himself to the ground. Staying low, he peered up from his position on the ground. A pair of creatures in the sky were battling each other with lightning. One looked like the strange half wolf, half man he had seen at the nightclub with Zatanna. The other was some sort of monster with claws and a thrashing tail.

Then a group of large new creatures came into view, tackling the first two. They were thick, with bald heads, and wore what looked like uniforms. Terrible piercing wails rose up all around Tim.

"What's going on?" he cried.

"We are at the final magical conflict of this age. You watch the last battle, child. Fifteen years into your future they will fight."

Then Tim's heart squeezed in his chest. He recognized the woman by the streetlight. "That's

Zatanna!" he shouted. She slumped against the light, dropping onto her knees. The light illuminated her wounds. She was bleeding. "She's hurt!" He scrambled to his feet. "We have to do something!"

"Why should we do anything?" Mister E asked, grabbing Tim's arm and stopping him. "This world is a possibility. Don't you understand? It hasn't happened yet. It may never happen. Or not like this."

Mister E still had Tim's arm; he dragged him farther along. Around the corner, Tim saw another horrible sight. John Constantine, also bleeding, slouched on the ground in a doorway.

"John!" Tim called. He yanked his arm out of Mister E's grip and charged over to his friend. He didn't care if he was breaking the rules. He had to help Constantine. John looked even worse up close. Tim knelt beside him.

"More ghosts?" John mumbled.

"Sort of," Tim answered. He glanced behind him and saw that Mister E stood a few feet away. "We're from the past. Can you see us?"

"I don't know. I think I may be delirious." John's eyes began to focus on Tim's face. He shook his head as if he was trying to clear it, then stared again. "Tim," he murmured. Then louder, "Timothy Hunter?"

"Yes!" Tim felt relieved that John recognized him.

"You little bastard," John spat. "I should have strangled you myself fifteen years ago. Or let them kill you. It would have saved us all a lot of grief. E had the right idea. I thought you were such a nice kid."

Tim sank back on his heels, stunned. He felt as if John had smacked him across the face. "Wh-What are you talking about, John? We're friends."

"What am I talking about? Do you see him? Up there? The leader of the opposition?"

John pointed a shaky finger toward the roof of a crumbling building. A tall, ominous man towered on the edge, sending out lethal lightning rays from the palms of his hands. He was surrounded by what looked like demons. Whatever they were, Tim knew they weren't human, and they reeked of evil. He could smell it from where he was.

"The guy in the blue suit?" Tim asked. He couldn't understand how any of this explained why John seemed to hate him now. "Did he do this to you?"

"That's you, Tim," John said. "What you've become."

"No!" Tim gasped. He clutched the lapels of

John's trench coat, his fingers opening and closing frantically. "It's not true. It won't happen like that!"

"Sorry, kid. It already happened. Oh yeah . . . and your pal Molly. You treat her right rotten. Disgraceful. I should have stopped that too."

"No," Tim moaned. He bent over John, his forehead touching the man's chest. He forced himself not to cry, not to throw up. "It can't be. It won't be."

"Hey, kid," John said.

Tim stood back up. John looked even paler now.

"Could you . . . could you light my cigarette, kid? The lighter is over there on the ground. I can't seem to move to reach it."

Tim hated seeing proud, free John Constantine like this. He crawled to the lighter, picked it up, and scurried back. He lit John's cigarette without even scolding him for smoking.

"Thanks, kid," John said. And then the light went out of his blue eyes.

Tim stumbled backward, horrified. He banged into Mister E and whirled around. "Is it true?" Tim demanded. "Is that me?"

"Yes."

Tim backed away from Mister E and charged down the alleyway, away from John, away from Zatanna, away from what John had told him about Molly. But it was a dead end. He faced a brick wall covered with graffiti, and knew the only way out of this nightmare was with Mister E. He'd never get home on his own. And that would mean he'd never be able to prevent this horrible future from happening.

Mister E approached Tim slowly, calmly, as if they had all the time in the world. "But this is not the only future. There are others in which you are Mage Supreme. Keeper of the Light. And there are an infinite number of options. In some of them, you are entirely uninvolved in this battle. And indeed there are futures in which this battle doesn't even occur."

Tim stared at Mister E. "I don't understand. So is this one more likely than the others?"

A nasty smile crossed Mister E's face. "No."

"Then why bring me here?" Tim demanded. "Are you just trying to upset me?"

"I felt you should see it. That is all."

Tim bit his lip, fighting the fury welling up inside him. "I don't like you, Mister E, or whatever your name is."

"You are not required to like me. I have shown you the triumph of evil as a precaution. Good is to be protected, evil eradicated. At all costs. That is my duty and my mission."

"I'm just a kid!" Tim shouted. "I shouldn't

have to see this stuff. Take me away from here!"

"Very well."

The world went black, as if lights blinked out. Mister E's voice floated toward Tim in the darkness. "Whatever occurred in that conflict— in any timeline in which it actually occurred—it will be the last brief flowering of magic of our era," Mister E said. "And your role may determine much."

Tim had never hated anyone as much as he hated the blind man beside him.

"I can feel the anger inside you," Mister E said. "I am quite used to it."

"Well, maybe if you cared more about people and their feelings, they wouldn't hate you," Tim spat.

"Let me tell you about people, Timothy," Mister E said. "My father taught me all I needed to know about people. That is why I'm blind."

"What?" Tim asked. He didn't see the connection.

"My father was wise. He knew that eyes could be misled—by charm, by shallow appearances, by glamour. I do not need my eyes. I see good and I see evil. Nothing else."

"But how did your father teach you that? And what does that have to do with your being blind?"

"He was a great man. He didn't want me to be blinded by shining surfaces. So he removed my eyes for me."

Tim stared, stunned. "That's sick!" he blurted.

"It has shaped my life," Mister E said. "And I am here to help shape yours."

Chapter Fourteen

"THEY'VE BEEN GONE a while," John Constantine needlessly pointed out. He dropped the cigarette to the ground and lit a new one as he ground out the old. Back to chain-smoking. That's what this lot did to him. "What exactly is E meant to be showing the kid, anyway?"

"The rise and fall of magic in the years to come," the Stranger explained. "But no more than a thousand years into the future. Beyond that, it becomes difficult to return."

"I would not question your judgment, sir, but why did you choose E?" Dr. Occult asked from his spot in the doorway. "I have heard disturbing things about him."

"One must use the vessels available," the Stranger replied. "Remember, he fought valiantly by us in Calcutta, and we'd still be battling the Cold Flame if he had not. And he is able—as we are not—to show the child the times yet to come."

"I still don't like it," Constantine grumbled.

The Stranger sighed. "Can you travel into the future?" he challenged.

"Only like everyone else, boss," Constantine admitted. "You know. One minute at a time."

"Where are we now?" Tim asked. "Or should I ask *when*?"

They stood on some sort of observation platform, looking out over an amazing city. It was like something out of a science fiction movie. Tall buildings gleamed, and crafts darted between them, as if people drove small spaceships instead of cars.

"There is no magic in this future," Mister E explained. "This is a world of science. Of technology. People do not choose magic, and therefore it doesn't exist."

This reminded Tim of Dr. Terry Thirteen. Constantine had said magic didn't exist for the professional debunker because he didn't believe in it.

"Where magic is concerned," Mister E continued, "there is always an initial decision, an initial willingness to let it into your life. If that is not there, then neither is magic."

"Oh."

"This civilization turned it down."

They moved quickly, and the scenes shifted in

front of Tim as if he were watching a fast-moving slide show, fast-forwarding through time: an orange-hued world that seemed to be on fire; next, a sky of spaceships populated by androids; tidal waves destroying a city—just like in Atlantis; new cities rising up. Tim felt dizzy, as he had when he flashed through the past with the Stranger. *But I must be getting used to this*, he thought. *I'm not going to throw up this time.*

They slowed down, and Tim realized that they were on a beach, beside a dark ocean. "Where are we now?" he asked.

"About forty centuries away from our own time. I have never traveled this far into the future before," Mister E said.

"It's so dark," Tim commented, then gave Mister E a quick embarrassed glance. "Oh, sorry, I forgot."

"No need to apologize. I wear my blindness proudly. I see more than you."

"You can't tell that it's dark, though."

"Look up," Mister E ordered. "Do you see that up there? That's the sun."

"That thing?" Tim stared at the dark orange circle in the sky. "How can the sun be out and it still be this dark?"

"Perhaps it has no heart to shine."

Tim looked up and down the beach. "I guess

there aren't any people anymore."

"You'd be wrong. There. Do you see them?" Mister E pointed to some figures climbing out of the water.

How does he do that? Tim wondered. *Are his other senses supermagnified to make up for being blind?* He glanced in the direction that Mister E pointed.

"But they aren't human, are they?" Tim squinted at the green, skeletal, distorted figures.

"They are all that's left. Perhaps fifty thousand people scrabbling a living on soil from which every nutrient has been leeched long since, from seas that barely support marine life. They live here in the dark."

"Why are they green?"

"Are they? I have no idea. Photosynthesis perhaps? Anyway, by now, concepts like science and magic have lost all meaning. There is only desperate survival."

"So this is how it ends," Tim said. "Some green skeletons digging for worms under a dying sun?"

"Possibly."

"Don't you know?"

"I have never traveled this far forward. I have only heard rumors."

"Oh. Well, there doesn't seem to be much to see here." He looked up at Mister E. "Shall we go back to our time, then?"

"No. We go on."

This time it was Dr. Occult who broke the tense silence back in London. "Shouldn't they be back by now?"

There was a thick pause. "Yes," the Stranger finally admitted.

"Is there a problem?" Constantine demanded.

"I am afraid so," the Stranger said. "They are lost to me. Wherever they have gone, it is so far into the future that I can no longer feel them. How about you, Dr. Occult?"

Dr. Occult shook his head. "They are completely gone."

"This is ridiculous!" Constantine exploded. "What are you saying? That they've headed off into the far future and there's nothing you can do to get them back?"

"Yes."

"I can't believe it! You trusted Tim to that loon? There are beds of kelp smarter than you, mate."

"I have made a mistake. I realize that. I apologize."

That only made Constantine even angrier. "That's not going to bring Tim back. He's just a kid. He trusted us to keep him safe. I don't—"

"Believe it," Dr. Occult finished for him. "We know. We also know that to err is human."

Constantine gave the Stranger a sideways glance. "If he's human, then I'm a toaster," he muttered.

"We must concentrate our efforts on getting them back," the Stranger said. "This bickering is futile."

"Can't you reach them?" Constantine asked. "Aren't there any gods or demons or anything you could send to get them back?"

"No," the Stranger replied. "But you have hit on something. Dr. Occult, the bird is Timothy's."

"Yes!" Dr. Occult took Yo-yo from John. Gazing deeply into the bird's yellow eyes, he addressed it in a commanding voice. "Listen to me, nightbird. Timothy, your master, where he is, wherever he might be, find him. Protect him. Help him." He tipped his head toward the Stranger. "My friend, lend me strength."

The Stranger nodded.

"Constantine, lend me will. Together you will both lend me faith."

They all concentrated on the bird for another moment.

"Now go!" Dr. Occult instructed.

Yo-yo flew off and vanished into the dark sky, the three men united in their hopes for the bird and its mission.

"I notice you didn't tell the bird to bring him back," Constantine commented.

Dr. Occult kept his eyes on the sky. "If he has gone that far into the future, it is unlikely that there is any force that can bring him back to us."

"So now what?" Constantine asked in a quiet voice.

The Stranger placed a hand on each of his companions' shoulders. "We wait."

Constantine sighed. "I wish you'd stop saying that."

Tim and Mister E floated in black, empty space. Tim was getting bored. Not much to see in the future, it seemed. And they didn't seem to be going anywhere. Just aimless floating.

"Where are we going now?" Tim asked. He was afraid he was starting to whine—like little kids on a road trip who kept asking "Are we there yet?" But he was growing impatient. Maybe if they had some destination in mind, he'd pay more attention. There'd be something to pay attention *to*, at least.

"To the end of time. To the very end."

"What happens then?"

"We will find out, won't we?"

Tim sighed. More riddles. He was fed up. He

was more than ready for this portion of the program to be over. If only he could change the channel or something.

"What do you see, child?" Mister E asked.

Tim peered around. Now that Mister E mentioned it, something *was* different—changing. His surroundings weren't just a flat black nothing anymore. "I don't know, it's so strange."

He tried to make sense of what he was seeing. Streaks of white light hurtled toward him but vanished as they came closer. "Everything in space is coming our way. All the stars are falling and the lights are going out. And it's a weird sort of color."

"What color?" Mister E asked eagerly. "Tell me."

"It's sort of a bluey purple. Whatever the color is at the end of the rainbow. Violet. All the stars, and galaxies."

"Blue shift!" Mister E declared.

"Pardon?"

"In our time," Mister E explained, "we have a red shift, as the stars and galaxies head away from us. Our universe is expanding. Now the universe is ending, and you're seeing the blue shift, as everything returns to the center."

"*Violet* shift, you mean," Tim corrected.

"What's happening now?" Mister E asked.

"Nothing," Tim replied. "There's nothing happening at all."

"This is how it ends, then," Mister E mused. "In darkness. In nothing. Interesting."

"Dead boring, if you ask me," Tim grumbled.

"This is the end, Tim. I can go no farther."

"Fine by me," Tim said, eager to go home. "Once you've been to the end of the universe, what else is there to do?" He scanned the darkness, the blankness. "I'd write my name on something, but there's nothing to write on. And no souvenirs to take home either." He faced Mister E again, who was floating nearby. "All right, then, let's go back."

"Very well. Come here. Let me hold your arm."

Tim moved toward Mister E, who was in an odd position now, one of his arms twisted behind his back. *Is he hiding something?* Tim wondered. *What could he possibly have picked up out here?* "What's that behind your back? What have you got?"

"I said, come here!"

Mister E lunged at him, grabbing the neck of his T-shirt. The sudden movement startled Tim, giving him no time to react.

"What's going on?" Tim demanded, struggling to get away. The strange gravity made it difficult to use his weight against Mister E and break free. "What's with you?"

"I don't want to hurt you, Tim," Mister E crooned. "I only want to protect you from the world, because it could corrupt you." He lifted Tim by his shirt into the air. Tim's eyes widened as he watched Mister E raise his other hand. He held a pointed wooden stake above his head. "Believe me, this is for your own good!"

Tim bit Mister E's hand, hard. It was enough to make the blind man release him with a yell. Tim fell backward, out of Mister E's reach.

It was as if Mister E didn't feel the wound, despite the blood gushing from his hand. "You cannot hurt me!" he cried. "Mine is the glory of rightness! Mine is courage unsullied!"

Tim was so disgusted he stopped being scared for a moment. "So you bring me here where there's absolutely no chance of anyone rescuing me? Yeah, that's courage all right!"

"Say good-bye, child."

Mister E somehow knew how to move more quickly than Tim did in this strange end-of-the-world atmosphere. The blind man seemed to be in front of him in an instant, one hand on his shoulder, the other rearing up, up, up. And then the stake plunged down.

Into Yo-yo.

The owl let out a shriek, and only then did Tim realize what had happened. Yo-yo had appeared out of nowhere and flew in front of him, to protect him. Yo-yo had taken the stake for him.

Blood and feathers flew everywhere and Yo-yo vanished, just . . . disappeared. Tim grabbed the bloody stake which was floating in the space in front of him. He hurled the wooden weapon at Mister E, knocking off the man's dark glasses.

Tim felt sick—from the blood, and Yo-yo's sacrifice. And now empty orbs in place of eyes stared out at him from Mister E's twisted face. Tim doubled over, breathing hard.

"You don't understand how powerful you might be," Mister E said. "I can see you, boy. You shine like a beacon in the darkness. I don't need eyes to find you. And I don't need a weapon. I can use my hands."

Tim felt powerful hands around his throat. He gasped for breath. He clutched at Mister E's fingers, trying desperately to pry them off his neck. He didn't think he could last much longer. The man was so strong—

"Stop that!" a voice ordered out of the darkness.

Mister E tumbled away, as if something had torn him from Tim.

Tim saw a strange man, wearing a dark cloak and hood, floating toward them. *Now what?* He rubbed his throat, swallowing a few times, and took in deep gulps of air.

"This is neither meet nor proper, behaving thus at the end of things."

The hooded man was now beside them. A lectern holding a thick book appeared. Had that been there all along? Tim wondered.

"You are Timothy Hunter," the man said. "And you are . . . ?"

"I call myself Mister E."

"Remarkable. Neither of you is in my book. One moment."

He consulted the large book on the lectern. "Ah yes. There is a footnote to this effect. I had almost forgotten. You are far from your own time, mortals."

A pretty, dark-haired woman appeared behind the man. "Hello, big brother." She wore all black, and lots of bangles and necklaces. Tim thought she looked like the kind of girl who'd have a tattoo and a belly-button ring. Like the Goth girl he knew at the council flats in London. She looked a little younger than Zatanna. What was she doing here? "Hello, you two."

Tim's head swam. Why were they floating around in space chatting as if asking directions to Heathrow, when just minutes ago Mister E had tried to kill him? And on top of it, the whole universe was ending! Tim gave up trying to figure out anything.

"You," exclaimed Mister E. He pointed at the girl. "I know you. You're Death. You've come for the boy, haven't you? Not me."

Tim gaped at her. This pretty girl who looked like she'd be at home at a rave was . . . Death? He looked at Mister E, who seemed panicked by her appearance.

Death smiled. It was a warm, friendly smile. "Hello, Tim. Hello E. No, I'm not here for either of you. I took both of you long ago. But it's nice to see you again. I'm here for the universe. And for my big brother, Destiny."

The man gazed at her fondly. "It sometimes seemed as if I would never turn the final page, never close my book for the last time. It is a relief to lay down my burden, sister. I thank you."

"'Bye, sweetums." The woman gave her brother a kiss on the cheek. Then he faded away like a reverse Polaroid snapshot.

Death turned to Tim and Mister E. "I can't let either of you stay here. You see, this really is it. The universe is over. You two have to go."

"Tim, this is yours," she said, and handed him his yo-yo, now a plastic toy again. He was glad Yo-yo hadn't vanished forever, even if it wasn't a living, breathing creature anymore. She held out

Mister E's dark glasses. "And I believe these belong to you."

Mister E snatched his glasses from her hand and put them on. "I must kill him," Mister E pleaded.

"No, that burden will not be yours," Death replied.

"Then what do I do?" He sounded lost.

"You, Mister E, will go back to your own time," Death said. "But you'll have to go the hard way, I'm afraid. Don't worry, you'll get there eventually."

"You don't understand," Mister E protested. "It's impossible. We're too far forward. We can't go back."

"Don't be silly. Of course you can. So get going, Mister E. You're walking back, step by step through the ages."

Death pointed a long pale finger past Mister E. Shoulders slumped, defeated, Mister E turned around and started walking, getting smaller and smaller, until he was nothing but a tiny dot.

"What about me?" Tim asked. "Do I have to walk all the way back through time too?"

"No," Death replied. "You've done enough traveling already. Close your eyes, Tim."

Again with the closed eyes. But he trusted this

darkly dressed, pretty woman. Since she was Death, and was sending him home, he figured he'd be okay. She didn't want to keep him. He'd survive. Wouldn't he?

Chapter Fifteen

"SO THIS IS IT, THEN," Constantine said wearily, hunching his shoulders against the damp London chill.

"Yes." The Stranger sounded just as weary.

"We really messed this one up."

"Not entirely," Dr. Occult argued. "We closed down the Brotherhood of the Cold Flame in India, after all. And they would have killed Tim."

"So instead we handed him over to a maniac who's done the job for them? Terrific."

"One day, another child will come," the Stranger said. "And when that day comes we will have learned from this."

"You are out of your tiny mind!" Constantine exploded. "If you think I am ever going to get involved in another of your bloody fiascoes—"

"Stop it!" Timothy Hunter shouted. "All of you."

The three men whirled around at the sound of

the boy's voice. They stared at him.

Tim grinned. *Finally, I got one over on them for a change*, he thought with satisfaction. "Yeah. I'm not dead. No thanks to you lot."

"Tim!" Constantine rushed over and clapped a large hand on Tim's back.

"Welcome home, child," the Stranger said.

"We are pleased to see you," added Dr. Occult.

"But how—"

"There was a woman there. At the end of time." Tim grinned up at John Constantine. "You probably would have liked her. Anyway, she sent me back here."

"And E?" asked the Stranger.

"He tried to kill me," Tim said. "I guess his punishment was that he'd have to find his own way back. The woman told him he would have to walk."

"It will be a long walk from eternity to here. He has my sympathies," the Stranger said.

"Even after he tried to kill Tim?" Constantine demanded.

"I'm afraid so," the Stranger admitted. "In some ways, E's road is the hardest of all."

"Where's your owl?" Dr. Occult asked.

Tim reached into his pocket and pulled out the yo-yo. "He saved my life when Mister E tried to kill me," Tim said. He stroked the plastic toy.

"The bird cared for you," Dr. Occult said.

Tim held out the yo-yo. "Can you bring him back?"

Dr. Occult looked sad, and shook his head. "No."

"Oh." Tim slipped the yo-yo back into his pocket and cleared his throat. He looked up at the three men. "So, I'm back. I've been all the way to the end of time, and I'm back."

"Timothy, you have seen what we have shown you," said the Stranger. "You have seen the past, you have met a handful of the present practitioners of the art. You have glimpsed some of the worlds that touch yours. You have seen the beginning and you have seen the end. Now yours is the decision."

Tim shifted his feet. He knew at some point they'd be asking him his choice, but he hadn't realized it would be so soon. He'd just gotten back. He hadn't had time to think.

"If you choose magic, you will never be able to return to the life you once lived," the Stranger reminded him. "Your world may be more . . . exciting. But it will also be more dangerous and unreliable. And once you begin to walk the path of magic, you can never step off it." The Stranger paused to let that sink in.

"Or you can choose the path of rationality," he continued. "Live in a normal world. Die a normal death. Less exciting, but safer. The choice is yours."

How could he choose? Tim felt cold from the bottom of his feet to the tips of his hair, cold through and through. Like fear—but deeper, more in his marrow than in his bones.

"I can't!" he blurted. He gazed down at his shoes. "I'm sorry. I appreciate what you've done for me. All the stuff I've seen. All that. But I've learned a lot of things."

He shoved his hands into his pockets and leaned back on his heels. He still couldn't quite face them. "The main thing I've learned is that it all has a price. I mean, you can get whatever you want, but it all has to be paid for. Like Merlin said. And I don't want to pay what it costs. I'm . . . I'm scared."

He took a deep breath, then finally looked up to meet their eyes. "I'm sorry. Are you angry?"

"It is your choice, Timothy," the Stranger assured him. "Always and forever your choice. It is not our place to approve or disapprove."

"Good-bye," Dr. Occult said.

"So long, kid," said John Constantine.

"'Bye," Tim mumbled. He looked down at his shoes again. When he looked back up, the Trench-coat Brigade was gone. He was left alone on the rainy deserted street, back in his own neighborhood, back in his old world. Back in London. Back in reality.

"Wait!" Tim cried. "I didn't mean it! I do want it! I do! I . . ." His voice trailed off as he realized what he'd done. And that it was too late to fix it.

Epilogue

Now THEY WERE THREE, the men in the trench coats. Constantine sat at the aged bar, smoking cigarette after cigarette.

"I said I didn't want anything to do with it," he groused. "I should have stuck to my guns." He looked at the other two men. Neither responded. "It's all been a bit of a washout, wouldn't you say?"

Dr. Occult and the Stranger sat in silence.

"Let's see." Constantine stood and paced, his feet kicking up the layers of dust that had been undisturbed until their recent visit. "Final score. Tim loses his one and only chance at magic, and we lose Mister E—not that I'm losing any sleep over that one."

"It's strange, Constantine," said Dr. Occult. "All the things I have heard about you. No one ever told me you were stupid."

"What? Hey, listen—"

"No. *You* listen. Listen and think." Dr. Occult waited for John to sit back down before continuing. "We told Timothy that we would give him a choice, did we not? And we did. He has seen magic. He knows it works. He has already walked a harder path than most initiates would ever dream of."

"Timothy's choice was not made a few moments ago," said the Stranger. "It was made when we first met."

"What?" Constantine looked at the two men, puzzled. Then he remembered. They had asked if he would go with them on the journey. *That* had been the choice. And Tim had said, "Yes. I'll come with you."

"You lied to him," John said.

"I did not lie to him, Constantine," the Stranger protested. "I told him it was his choice to make, and it was. I asked him if he wanted to take this journey. He did."

A small smile crept onto Constantine's rugged face. "And people accuse *me* of being manipulative. Now what?"

"For now, I think we ought to wait," said the Stranger. "Observe the boy."

"Just wait and see?" said Constantine. "Where have I heard that little refrain before?"

"We will wait." The Stranger nodded.

"And we will see," finished Dr. Occult.

The boy who had the potential to become the most powerful human adept in all history stumbled home in the rain. Miserable, cold, wet, hungry, and disappointed. Disappointed into a kind of numbness.

He arrived at his flat and opened the door to the familiar gloom. The only light came from the television set. His father sat in front of it, surrounded by beer bottles.

"Tim?" his father called as he slunk past him, heading for the stairs.

"Yeah?"

"Have a good day, son?"

Tim went into the living room. "How long have I been gone, Dad?"

"What is this? Twenty questions? A few hours."

"Didn't I phone you from San Francisco? Or from Brighton, with Auntie Blodwyn?"

"Don't be a pillock," his dad scolded. "No one's phoned since you've been out. So what did you do, then? Where did you go? Seems to me like I'm the one who should be asking the questions as to your whereabouts."

"Nowhere. I was just out. You know."

"Pull up a chair. This is a good one. Great bit

at the end, where they drive these minis all through Rome."

"No thanks. I think I'll go up to my room for a bit."

"I'll put on a pizza for dinner, then."

Tim climbed the stairs to his room. It seemed small. Cramped. Dead. He pulled the yo-yo from his pocket and gazed at it. Had it happened at all?

He flipped open his journal. Usually he felt better if he could write it all out. He grabbed a pen . . .

Nothing.

He felt washed in anger; he could drown in it. How could they do that to him? Putting on all that pressure! Dragging him all over the place, from the beginning of time to the end. Showing him worlds with so little explanation. How could he be expected to choose after what they'd put him through?

"I don't need you lot!" he shouted.

They had offered him so much, confused him, changed him, then abandoned him. Well, he'd show them! "I don't need you at all. You or anyone. All I need—is to *believe*!"

Tim's hand tingled, as if he'd gotten an electric shock. The yo-yo burst into a new shape, a new form.

It was an owl again!

Yo-yo flew out Tim's open window and vanished into the night.

Tim stumbled backward, gasping. *Did I . . . ? How did . . . ?*

Then he knew . . . knew everything. He threw his arms into the air. "Magic!" he cried.

Magic.

**The journey continues
in *The Books of Magic 2:* BINDINGS**

*And so it shall come to pass,
A mortal child,
Like his father before him,
Shall venture into the realm.*

*A child at the brink of discovery
Shall arrive in the Fair Lands.
When she herself is at the brink
Her hope lies in his hands.*

Need answers need.

*Like his father before him,
He will have the power of transformation,
But while his father transforms in the flesh,
shedding the human at will,
The child will transform destiny.*

THE FALCON'S WINGS WERE POWERFUL, and the bird shot rapidly into the sky. Tamlin, the Queen's Falconer, shaded his brown eyes against the sun to peer up at his charge. Satisfied by its soaring circles, knowing the bird would not attempt a getaway, Tamlin's attention turned inward. He could no longer ignore the pressing questions that nagged at him.

Could it be true? he wondered. The prophecies from long ago—he had put no store in them. But now he could not keep from thinking about the possibilities. Nor could he keep his mind off the child who had come here, to this place called Faerie, and bested the Queen at one of her own games.

Tamlin had only caught a glimpse of the boy from the realm of mortals, but he had not forgotten him. A lad who could hold his own with the Queen would be remembered.

But could Timothy Hunter, who briefly visited the realm of the Fair Folk, be the child of the prophecy? If he were—and if the prophecy were true—there would be consequences for Tamlin, the Queen, even for Timothy himself. Because of this, Tamlin did not know even his own heart— what to hope or whether hope was possible. Tamlin did not want to be deceived again. He had been deceived too easily in the past by the glamours of Faerie.

The falconer sighed. There were too many times he had allowed himself to be deceived by this land. Faerie had offered untold pleasures: beauty, joy, and delight. A caressing breeze, sparkling brooks, beckoning lakes, wild forests dappled and mysterious. But that was before everything changed. *One believes what one wants to*, Tamlin mused, *and Faerie herself seems to encourage self-delusion, finding secret ways to make it easier to accept what should be unacceptable. She has the power to conjure illusion and create delusion.* Tamlin's long tenure in this world had made that painfully apparent.

Tamlin raised his gloved hand to signal the falcon he was training to return. *And what of the Queen?* Tamlin wondered. *She is so practiced at pretense it would be hard to glean what she knows of Faerie, of the prophecy, of anything.* The majestic bird swooped down and landed neatly on Tamlin's wrist. Its talons gripped the thick leather of his glove. Tamlin spoke soothingly to the bird as it preened, then lowered a hood over the bird's head. "You and I are the same," he told the bird. "We soar to our heart's content, but we have only the illusion of freedom."

Tamlin scanned the horizon. It pained him to see what had become of the royal hunting grounds. Where once majestic trees had sheltered myriad animals, now there stood withered, gnarled deformities. Beyond them were the devastated valleys, the choked and thirsty ground cracked and dead. Like all of Faerie.

He knew he must act, and soon.

Titania, Queen of Faerie, stood at the low marble wall that surrounded a patio behind the palace. The twilight sky matched her mood as it transformed the pale and placid scene into something darker and intense.

That child, she thought, *that child who arrived from the realm of the mortals. And yet—his power.* It simply made no sense to her. Unless . . .

Have I been deceived? she wondered, her golden eyes narrowing. She did not see the scene before her, the courtiers strolling the paths, sprites making sport on the crystalline lake, the pretty flitlings hovering nearby awaiting her command. What she saw was treachery, duplicity, and danger. She, too, was distracted by the ancient prophecies. All those years ago— What had *truly* happened to the child? She had thought he had died, had been told of it, but had not witnessed it herself. She should not have been so foolish; but she had placed more stock in trust then, and some would say trust is cherished by fools. Today it would have been different, and she would not be facing this . . . this astonishing possibility.

This could be a boon, she realized. Anger over the possibility that the child of the prophecy was still alive, over being lied to, should not cloud her recognition of the advantage the child could pose. But at the same time, the prophecy might not be true at all. And the child, despite her suspicions, may still very well be gone.

Trust. Despite her hesitation, trust was what she had to count on, and it was such a tricky thing. Tamlin had never lied to her, more's the pity. There were certainly times when she wished that he had. In the past, he'd hidden things from her but when asked a direct question he inevitably gave her a direct answer, even if that answer put him in danger of her wrath.

Yes. He was the only one she could ask, the only one who could find out the truth. But how would he react to this news? *He may have already solved this riddle*, she realized. In which case, she wanted to be included in whatever knowledge he had.

She shut her eyes and felt the breeze growing cooler as the sun fell below the horizon.

"Come, my Falconer." She summoned Tamlin with her mind by picturing him. She heard a flutter of wings and smiled.

"Why have you called me?" a growling voice demanded.

Titania slowly opened her eyes. Tamlin—tall, lean, muscular; the betrayed and betrayer; her beloved and despised one—stood before her. His straight brown hair hung to his shoulders, framing his angular face. Adversary and only true friend. They had so much history between them it hung thick and heavy in the air whenever they were together.

Now that he was here, she was unsure how to
proceed. With everyone else—even with her husband King Auberon—she did as she would without a thought, not a twinge of concern about what
she might be asking or doing. Yet with Tamlin she
was humbled. She wanted his approval, particularly because he rarely gave it.

But she didn't look at him; instead, she kept
her eyes fixed in front of her. She noticed a few of
the tiny flitlings buzzing nearby and waved them
away. Gossip would not be welcome. She nodded
at the two armed servants who had placed themselves discreetly just beyond earshot. There were
always several bodyguards around. It would
attract too much attention if she dismissed
them—it would be too obvious that this was a personal matter.

"I have been wondering . . . about that boy,"
she said. She kept her voice light, as if this were
nothing but idle curiosity.

"What boy?" Tamlin asked.

This time she looked at him, an eyebrow
raised. She was letting him know that she was
aware he knew precisely what boy she was talking about.

"Ah." Tamlin said. "The mortal one, who
made his way into this world not long ago."

"Yes, him." She sat on the wall, her back to

the lawn. She spotted her jester, Amadan, peering down at them from her bedchamber window in the turret. What was he doing up there? Spying, she assumed. She made sure Amadan knew that she saw him. She might need him, but she wanted him to remember who was in charge. That flitling was small, but he held most of the court in his thrall, always scheming, stirring up intrigues within intrigues.

She smoothed her long skirt over her knees. The light breeze made the translucent pastel chiffon layers flutter. "I am glad he was brought to me."

Tamlin nodded, waiting for her to play her hand.

"I sense great power in Timothy Hunter," Titania said. "He bears watching. I want you to bring him back here. Now."